PLATINUMS

SOPHIA BORZILLERI

ISBN 978-1-64300-002-2 (Paperback)
ISBN 978-1-64300-003-9 (Hardcover)
ISBN 978-1-64300-004-6 (Digital)

Illustrations by: Kaya Tinsman

Covenant Books, Inc.
11661 Hwy 707
Murrells Inlet, SC 29576
www.covenantbooks.com

CONTENTS

1

The Surprise Present

"Chris!" his mom called from downstairs. It was a beautiful Sunday morning, and Chris was in bed staring into space. He knew what was going to happen next.

"Christopher Matthew, if you're not down here in five minutes, you will lose electronics for a week!"

Chris loved electronics more than a few extra minutes of sleep, so he fell out of bed and got dressed. Chris Porter was a tall boy with dark hair. At sixteen and in tenth grade, he was pretty happy most of the time, except when he didn't want to do something. Chris sleepwalked downstairs, almost hitting his head on his mom's hanging spider plant in the process.

"There you are!" His mother sounded annoyed. "Today is Cousin Mary's birthday party." Chris's mom usually acted like this on these types of occasions. She looked a little intimidating from afar, but once you got to know her, she was pretty nice.

"I know. I didn't forget." He had a quick breakfast before his fidgety mom hurried him out the door and down the street. "Do I really have to go?" Chris asked.

"We are literally three seconds away from her house! You should go to support her!" Chris's mom exclaimed. He knew what

SOPHIA BORZILLERI

she really meant was, "Go so you don't make me look like a bad aunt."

Chris did not like the idea one bit, but he thought through it some more and decided that he might as well go and get cake. This raised his spirits, especially when he remembered how delicious his aunt's cakes were. When they arrived, he saw his cousin talking to a few of her friends. Her name was Mary Christianson. She was in ninth grade, which made her a little younger than Chris. She had sandy-blond hair with welcoming hazel eyes that were perfect accessories to her floral blue dress and silver flats.

"Hey, Chris!" she called from across the lawn.

Darn it! Chris thought. His plan was to stay invisible. Unfortunately, his plans never worked. So he wasn't surprised when Mary and her preppy companions giggled and sauntered toward him. They circled around him and did exactly what Chris was not looking forward to—whispering to each other about him. It was obvious. It was even more so when they threw some more giggles, squeals, and exaggerated smiles into their not-so-private conversation.

"Um, hi!" said Chris. "I was just going over to the wonderful establishment that is the snack area, so bye." He backed away slowly from the giddy girls and turned a corner. Chris sighed with relief when he knew he was safe and vowed to act as invisible as possible without arousing suspicion.

When Aunt Colleen announced it was time for races and games, he debated his few choices, analyzed the pros and cons of each, and decided it would be safe to stay and watch the festivities from afar. If anyone asked, he'd fake a hurt arm or a sore throat, even though he considered himself pretty athletic and a heck of a good guesser. To his extreme disappointment, Aunt Colleen took him by the shoulders and steered him toward the frenzied crowd.

"This is a relay race," his aunt shouted above the roar. "You need to run to the banner, circle it five times, then run back as fast as you can, and tag the next person in line."

6

The contestants split into two teams of ten and voted for a "super cool" team name. Chris was on Mary's team. Most of their team was pretty athletic, so he felt a little better. Patrick came up with the name, Spicy Dragons. Chris happened to like dragons, so he went with it. At least it was better than the other team's name, the Terrifying Turtles. No explanation there.

"Ready . . . set . . . GO!" Aunt Colleen shouted.

Mary took off running with a serious face molded on, surging toward the cones as if her life depended on it. Chris would have actually paid attention to the race if he weren't interrupted by a loud booming voice that wailed, "You are blind now, but you will know your destiny soon enough!"

"Chris, wake up!" Mary shook him with worry. "What's wrong with you?" she asked again, this time sounding more annoyed than worried.

Chris felt dazed and weak. He was quite surprised to find himself sprawled out on the tickly grass of the Christiansons' lawn. When he was asked about the cause of his unexpected plunge, he didn't want to risk sounding like a crazy kid with an imaginary friend problem so he just shrugged. It was in that moment when he wished his best friend Karl were there to calm him down and tell him reassuring things like he didn't have sunstroke, he didn't need to go to therapy, and it was no big deal to hear a voice in his head. Karl would also say that Chris was not allowed to go to any more parties as long as he was in the recovery stage. That was one of the reasons why Karl was his best friend. Of course, he had other friends too, but there was something about Karl that Chris could trust and connect with more than anyone else. Other people just didn't understand him like Karl did.

"Cake time!" Chris heard his aunt shout out to everyone in the vicinity. Cake had been the furthest thing from Chris's mind, but he was hungry, and his mother would probably scowl if he didn't participate in this birthday tradition. He zombie-walked over and sat as far away from the candles as possible while they sang "Happy Birthday." He had always had an irrational fear of fire. With his luck today, he wasn't going to take any chances. It was time to open presents. *An Xbox, new clothes, a hairstyling kit, and a life-size cardboard cutout of Justin Bieber,* Chris guessed to himself. There were at least ten more gifts, but he didn't want to guess all of them and spoil his fun. As Mary opened her Xbox and hairstyling kit, Chris spotted a black metal box about the size of two bricks. Mary started unwrapping her Justin Bieber cutout when Chris realized that the box had no bow or tag on it. Chris inched closer and saw a strange symbol on the lid. It was a big circle with one triangle facing up and one down. There were also two lines curving up that protruded from the circle like antennae. Chris was suspicious of the mysterious black box, but he inched back to his original spot and tried to forget about it.

"That one next!" Mary pointed to the black box in the stack of presents. She opened it and pulled out a . . . note. "What?" Mary said, looking slightly stunned. "What?" she said again. She read the note to herself and frowned. All eyes were on her. "Is this a joke?" No one claimed the strange gift; so she folded up the note, put it back in the box, and set it aside. Then she cleared her throat and continued with her presents.

Chris could hardly sleep that night. He tossed and turned every couple minutes, thinking about the box's vibe. More importantly, he wondered what the note said. He knew it had to be something significant because of Mary's spooked reaction. He lay there for a while until he got a crazy idea. He would talk to the voice! Oh, where was Karl when he needed him.

"Oh, mighty voice!" Chris felt ridiculous. But in his defense, it was nighttime and a person is never quite himself when it's dark out. "What does this mean? What is happening?" He waited for an answer.

"So now you want to talk to me?" boomed the voice.

Chris jumped so hard the bed creaked. The voice began to speak a prophecy.

> *Four will venture to find an adventure.*
> *Three with a tool to help cross the wide pool.*
> *One will pursue a talent hid,*
> *While another gets caught in a pyramid.*
> *One finds riches in the mountain pass,*
> *While another finds the most valuable treasure at last.*

Chris was stunned. Was this a dream? If so, he would like to wake up soon. Then he said to the voice, "Did you make that up 'cause it really didn't rhyme too well."

"If you don't believe me, find out for yourself," the voice answered.

Chris's eyelids got heavy, and the voice faded from his mind. He let his eyelids droop and went to sleep.

Beep! Beep! Beep!

It was Monday. Chris's alarm clock sounded as he dressed more quickly than usual and fixed his hair. He was never excited for Mondays, but today he had two things to look forward to. One, he could finally talk to Mary face-to-face about the weird note. Two, it was the last day of school. He had expressed his disapproval with the school for scheduling the last day on a Monday, but no finger was lifted to change it, so unfortunately, he and all his peers were stuck with another worthless day. Chris slammed his alarm clock again and bolted down the stairs. His mom was making breakfast, his favorite, toast with a dollop of whipped cream on top. He ate at lightning speed, stuffing food in his mouth while talking to his mom about Mary's party. Both he and his mother had no idea why he was so chatty, but they just went with it. At school, Chris skidded to a stop when he saw Mary.

"What did the note say? What did it say?"

"One, why are you so excited to see me? Two, you really scared me. And three, why do you care so much about the note?"

"You are going to think I'm crazy, but there's this creepy voice that's been talking to me ever since Sunday afternoon. That's why I spaced out at the party."

Mary looked surprised. "Me too," she said, gripping her books.

2

THE THIRD COMPANION

Chris was beside himself with glee. Apparently, he wasn't the only one who heard a creepy man's voice in his head.

"How long exactly have you been hearing the voice?" asked Chris.

"A day before the party," Mary answered.

"Well, what did he say to you?" Chris had a thousand questions he wanted to ask, but because of the time, he decided to ask just the top one hundred. "Did the voice quote a badly rhyming prophecy to you or just to me?"

Mary began to recite the exact prophecy that Chris had heard the night before! Mary stopped.

"So wait a sec. You and I are two of the people who are supposed to go on this quest thingy?" she asked, tilting her head. "What if it's magic? I mean, it would make sense, right? How many people can say that they've heard a voice talk to them and not be completely insane?"

Just then, the bell rang.

"Gotta go," Mary said. "I'll talk to you at lunch."

Chris's school was called Cleveland High School. It was a decent size with about two hundred kids in each grade. It was a public school, but the kids had to wear uniforms every Wednesday to "show school spirit." Most of the teachers were nice, except for Mrs. Pond and Dr. Rockwell. Chris was "lucky" enough to get Dr. Rockwell for homeroom, math, *and* science. Dr. Rockwell was so fond of his title that if anyone called him "mister" or even "sir," they would be banned from something.

Every class felt like the world was moving in slow motion, and the teachers were talking at snail speed. It didn't help that he was so jittery. A few kids noticed and told him more than once to sit still. Finally, it was lunch. He had lost some energy tapping his foot on the ground and falling out of his seat (twice), so he got into the cafeteria not as fast as he would've liked.

Mary spotted Chris and headed toward him until she was sure that they could converse without the attention of the other students.

"The piece of paper that I received in the box was the same prophecy spoken to you last night." She paused for a second and leaned in even closer. "I didn't tell you this earlier, but inside my box, there was a bright-blue hair clip. I unclipped it, and I swear I saw it transform into a sword." She demonstrated with her pencil to an all-focused Chris. "I looked again and nothing was there, but I know I saw it so clearly!"

"A hair clip became a sword?" Chris asked, raising his eyebrow.

"Maybe there will be some nasty pirates that attack us or something, but I know we will be safe because I have a magic hair clip sword!"

Just then, Karl walked up, shaking his head. "You're not going to believe this, but I just heard the weirdest thing."

"We know. Us too," said Mary. "So what did our little croaky-voiced life interpreter say to you?"

"Well, I walked out the door this morning and saw a black metal box sitting on my front porch. When I looked inside, I saw a tiny boat that was so realistic, I swear I heard seagulls. Then that raspy voice came out of nowhere and said, 'If you fail, your friends will fail.'"

Chris thought that over. *Karl's got a boat and a note. He is totally part of this quest, and I am 100 percent fine with that arrangement.* When school finally ended, Chris walked home with Mary and Karl. They talked about all the adventures they were going to have together with Karl's boat and Mary's death clip.

"I have to go," Chris sighed when they reached his house.

"Bye, dude." Karl waved to his friend.

"Okay. See you soon," called Mary.

Chris walked to his front steps, humming a happy tune. He was so lost in thought by the time he got to the front door that he almost tripped on something. There on his doorstep sat a box that looked an awful lot like the one Mary received at her party. It was a black metal box with a symbol on top.

3

An Unexpected Visit

Chris threw off his backpack and dove for the box. He opened it up to find a rusty old compass and a note just like the one Mary described. He picked up the note and read it aloud.

"Could you take on evil alone?" *Not likely*, Chris thought.

He put the note back in the box and carried it into the living room where his mother was reading one of her fashion magazines. He wanted to talk to her about everything that had been going on, but he didn't think his mom would believe him if he told her that he had a voice in his head telling him a life-changing prophecy. Plus, his mom knew that he read fantasy books, so she would link it with them. Nevertheless, he decided to give it a shot.

"Hey, Mom," he began. "Can I tell you something?"

His mom looked up from her magazine and smiled up at him. "Okay," she said and put down her *Vogue*. She looked at him with an expression like she was ready to hear whatever crazy story he had in store for her today. Chris thought that one of the best things about her was that she listened to him no matter how ridiculous or insane he sounded.

He took a deep breath. "Since Mary's party, I've been hearing this strange voice in my head that told me I was 'blind now' but soon I would 'know my destiny.' Then later, it recited a prophecy about four people going on a quest." Chris realized how childish and unmanly he sounded. After a short pause, he continued with his story. "I also received the prophecy in writing today. Here." Chris handed the paper to his mom. He sat down while his mom studied the note and watched as her expression changed from happiness to concern. He cleared his throat and went on. "I only know of three people that this has happened to so far—me, Karl, and Mary. We are on the lookout for the fourth person since according to this, there is one more coming."

"Chris," his mom began, "there are so many things I should probably tell you—"

Wait, what? Chris thought. She was acting like she was expecting this to happen, like she had been waiting for years.

"I was wondering when you, Karl, and Mary would discover your destiny." She stood up and grabbed Chris's shoulders, squeezing them slightly. "Everything is going to be okay. I will call their parents and have everyone over to discuss the situation." It almost seemed like she was reassuring herself more than her son. Chris did not know what to think, but as his mother went to get her phone, she turned back to face him again. She added, "The fourth will be arriving shortly."

Just ten minutes later, Karl, Mary, and all five parents were in the Porters' living room, sitting uncomfortably on any piece of furniture they could find with emotionless expressions plastered on their faces.

"We all know why we're here," Mrs. Porter said, being the first person to break the silence once everyone had assembled.

Chris mumbled under his breath, "I don't."

"It is time for our children to fulfill their destinies." Chris's mom paused for a moment. "Time for our children to defeat our adversary. The enemy has already begun his plan of attack, so the kids must begin their journey immediately. They must be alert, cautious, and cunning at all times to complete this mission successfully."

"Can I ask a ques—" Chris got cut off by his mom. What was she now, a spy?

"Please, just let me finish." she replied firmly. "As you know, your dad and I started dating in college. What you don't know is that soon after we graduated, your dad, whom you know as Klayton, told me his true identity. He explained that his real name was Klayric and that he was from the magical country of Lamin. Since he had completed his degree, he needed to return to his homeland. My sister Colleen and I decided to go with him. Klayric and I got married and began a new life in Lamin. We lived there for about three years before you were born. In the meantime, we met Karl's parents, my sister got married, then Mary and Karl were born. When the evil sorcerer Erex threatened the safety of Lamin, we decided to raise you three kids back here in the States. Erex was eventually defeated and went into exile but . . " Mrs. Porter drifted off.

Aunt Colleen had been waiting patiently the entire speech. Chris forgot she was even there, so he was a bit startled when she spoke. "Haven't you forgotten an important detail, Nancy?"

Mrs. Porter sunk down into her favorite chair and took a few moments to look into the eyes staring at her before speaking again. "Right, your real names. You will use them always when you go on the quest. Karl, your true name is Zennith. Mary, yours is Aidryan, and Chris, your name is—"

Ding-dong! The doorbell rang.

Chris's mom jumped up to answer it. "Ah, Maylis is here," she said.

Chris decided to get up and follow her. He had an irrational fear that this Maylis person was a psychopath. He let his mom open the door and was completely surprised. Standing in the doorway was a lanky, dark-haired boy who appeared to be around the same age as the other kids. He had a lighthearted smile on his face, which made Chris feel a little less paranoid. The only thing he deemed extraordinary about him, besides his weird name, was his clothes. He wore a dark cloak that hung from his shoulders, half covering an outfit that was completely outdated.

"Hey, everyone!" he called. He sauntered past Chris and crossed to the living room where all the parents looked excited to see him. The kids, however, were clueless. The parents got up and greeted him like an old friend.

After a few minutes of catching up and a few wow-you-have-grown-so-much tears, Chris's mom led Maylis over to the inquisitive kids and proceeded to introduce him.

"Chris, Mary, Karl, this is Maylis. He grew up in Lamin."

"Nice to meet you. My name is Mar—Aidryan. *Whoops*, almost forgot my new name." She turned to Chris with a concerned expression. "Speaking of which, Chris, your mom never told us what *your* real name is."

Chris was thinking about everything that had happened over the past few days and just couldn't be bothered to feel more anxiety about a name, so he abruptly left the conversation and sat down. The prophecy was real, he couldn't escape it. Then he thought, *It's better to embrace the adventure then to suppress the fear and get absolutely nowhere.* His eyes glanced up at Mary. She rolled hers at him and went back to talking to the mystery guy. A few minutes later, Mary was pleased to see Chris standing beside her with a forced but pleasant smile. He had taken his own advice and nodded to Mary, which said that he would be all in from now on. Mary smiled back and let Chris and Maylis talk for a little bit.

"I was just telling your cousin why I have come to see you," Maylis began. "I arrived here from Lamin to get you prepared for the journey ahead of you. I have been chosen to be your quest coach, so I'm basically like a sword-fighting, magic-using hero maker."

"Cool! So we have to train to go on the quest?" Karl asked eagerly.

"If you plan to survive," Maylis affirmed. "We will meet tomorrow morning at—"

Mary raised her hand.

"Okay, Aidryan. We will meet at your house at 9:00 a.m. sharp! I will talk to your parents to tell them what we have decided. By the way, your parents knew me when I was a baby so that was the reason for the whole . . " He demonstrated by hugging himself. "Oh, and one more thing. Chris, did your mother tell you your name?"

"It might have slipped her mind. I'll ask her."

"Good. Be sure to come prepared with it tomorrow when we begin training." Maylis said quick goodbyes to his new clients and grabbed his cape from the coat rack. He spoke briefly to the parents about the training schedule, then headed out the door.

"We are going to fight epic battles and find treasure and maybe even learn some magic spells with the help of our very own *quest coach*!" Karl exclaimed.

All three exploded in laughter.

"Okay, settle down, you guys," Mrs. Porter said. "Maylis told us your training schedule. You will meet at Mary's house six days a week for a month to give you enough time to prepare." She glanced back to the other parents to confirm the arrangement. "Maylis will bring everything you will need, supplies wise, to your training session tomorrow. Karl, Chris, pack your things. You are sleeping at Mary's house tonight."

"Yay!" They all yelled in unison. They jumped up and down as if their five-year-old selves had returned. They were celebrating hard when Chris realized that he didn't know his name and he was expected to come prepared with it tomorrow.

"Hey, wait, Mom! What's my other name? We got interrupted the last time you tried to tell me."

His mom sighed, "Right. You must be careful who you tell your name to. It is a very special one that should not be thrown around carelessly." Her face was more serious than ever before. "Your name is Dagon, prince of Lamin. It is time for you to defeat Erex and rule beside King Klayric, your father."

THE FIRST TRAINING SESSION

Beep! Beep!

Mary's alarm clock buzzed for several minutes until Mary, Karl, and Chris finally got out of bed and sat down to a quick breakfast of toast and bacon. They ate until they were stuffed so they wouldn't be hungry for their first day of training.

"This is going to be amazing!" Chris announced.

Mary and Karl agreed. It really was going to be amazing.

"I cannot wait to train with a sword, learn how to use magic spells, and wield them against you guys," added Karl.

Mary rolled her eyes at Karl. "So, Chris, you're a prince, the prince of our homeland, Lamin?"

"I guess." Chris shrugged, trying not to make it a big deal. But yes, it kind of was a big deal in the sense that the father he didn't know was actually a king. Chris would never have guessed his family was important in any sort of politically powerful way.

Then Mary said, "So this Erex guy is the adversary we are supposed to defeat?"

Chris knew it was extremely unlikely that four teenagers could vanquish a powerful sorcerer, but he didn't want to disappoint her.

"Now that Maylis is training us, I'm sure we will kick his butt."

That seemed to satisfy Mary. With that, they finished their breakfast and went outside to meet Maylis in Mary's backyard. The property had a breathtaking view of the summer sun. Yellow daisies swayed along the edge of the white-painted fence, and the neatly cut grass felt tickly on their feet.

"Ahoy there! Ready for your first lesson?"

Maylis stood suspended about fifteen feet in the air. Mary, Chris, and Karl heard his voice but had to look around for a few seconds before seeing him.

"*Whoa!*" Chris said.

Maylis descended toward the young heroes who were still experiencing a pinch of shock. Maylis faced them and began his first lesson.

"We will start by remembering to call each other and ourselves by our Laminian name." He pointed at everyone allowing them to say their Laminian name aloud. He stopped when he saw Chris.

Chris hesitated but took a deep breath and spoke. "My name is Dagon, prince of Lamin."

Maylis stepped back and bowed. He said some sort of pledge while he was bowing. The words reminded Dagon of the pledge that they do at school. He was going to have to get used to these acknowledgments. Maylis stood up and continued with his lesson.

"Today we get uniforms. You must use them exclusively for training."

Cool. Dagon loved getting uniforms for some reason. They made him look important and feel like part of a team. Plus, they were imported from Lamin. Maylis went over to a trunk resting on the neat lawn. He pulled out three outfits: yellow, blue, and green. He handed the yellow one to Aidryan, the green one to Zennith, and the blue one to Dagon. Maylis had on a red uniform with a trainer's badge on his left shoulder. Every uniform looked about the same, except for the color, and each had a radiant yellow sun stitched on the back. When they finished loving their new clothes, Maylis waved his hand in a circular motion and three colorful tents appeared in front of them.

"These tents," he said, "correspond with the color of all your equipment. When you are finished dressing, bring your wands out with you."

The friends smiled. Three . . . two . . . one. They ran at full speed, eager to begin. Surprisingly, the uniforms fit as if they were made specifically for them. They were just the right size and fitted to their waist with sleeves that were just the right length. As they looked around the room, they noticed the amazing equipment that lined the walls.

Zennith was very surprised when he saw a helmet sitting on a table with other battle gear. If this quest had to do anything with fighting, especially against the mighty Aidryan and Dagon, then this was going to be the shortest month of his life.

Dagon, Aidryan, and Zen came out of their tents with wands in hand to meet the awaiting Maylis.

"Okay, today we will dip our toes in a little magic."

They studied their wands. Each was very smooth and had a polished translucent crystal on one end.

Maylis said, "Let's start with some simple spells, like making fire and water appear out of thin air and, my personal favorite, levitation spells." Maylis pointed his wand at a bowl sitting in the grass. "*Shastalega!*" Instantly, water filled up the bowl. "You can control the amount of water using the power of your mind." He walked over and dumped out the bowl for the next person. Everyone was intrigued. "Now you try!"

Aidryan went first. She hesitated but quickly got over it. "*Shastalega!*"

Sure enough, water began to fill up the bowl. Everyone clapped, and Maylis dumped out the water again. "Good. This is going to be easy." Maylis smiled. He pointed to Zennith.

Zennith was usually the person who jumped at the chance to try new things, but magic was a very different matter. Now he was afraid he would screw up horribly and the world might implode because of his lack of know-how. "*Shastalega!*" Water filled up the bowl in the same manner as Aidryan's spell. "Yay, I did it!" Zennith happily flicked his wand around at his victory.

"Okay, Dagon. Let's see what our prince can do," Maylis said, facing him.

"*Shastalega!*"

At first nothing happened. Then they heard a noise in the distance that sounded like running water. An immense wave came pounding into view.

"*Marmadin!*" Maylis yelled as he jumped in front of the wall of water, turning it into ice not ten feet away from the companions. Maylis steadily turned to Dagon. "Well, you seem to know how to make water appear."

A still stunned Dagon answered modestly, "Yeah, I guess I kinda do."

Maylis quickly faced the ice wall he made and waved his wand at it until it melted into the grass.

"On to the next spell, shall we? Creating fire. Please be very careful." He looked pointedly at Dagon, who was trying to appear as innocent as only a very guilty person could manage. Three torches sprouted up from the ground, one in front of each of the students. "You will light these torches all at once," Maylis commanded. "Point your wand at the torch and say, '*Hasanta!*'"

The three friends got ready, practicing flicking their wands correctly. They readied their stances.

"Ready? One . . . two . . . three!" Maylis counted down.

Shortly after, flames came bursting out of two of the three torches. Zennith tried again but still no flame flickered at the top of his.

"What's that smell?" Chris wondered when he inhaled the unmistakable smell of smoke. A moment later, they saw fire erupt from the ground and form a flaming ring around them.

"Oookay. Well, I guess I did the spell correctly," muttered Zennith.

"A little too correctly, Zen," Maylis said as he pointed his wand, and the fire circle disappeared. "Well, now we know what hidden talent *you* possess."

Zennith couldn't help but grin a little. He had never had a hidden talent before.

Maylis took this moment to tell the young wizards a little more about Laminian history.

"Many years ago witches and wizards came from all over the world to the kingdom of Lamin. Each had a special talent of fire, levitation, transformation, and water. Eventually, they settled into city-states, one for each type of talent. Everyone had only one special talent, except for one wizard who happened to be Dagon's great-great-grandfather. He was the first of your ancestors to be king."

Maylis clapped his hands to signal the beginning of the next skill. "Next, we will learn how to shoot arrows and sword fight."

5

THE FANTASY MUSEUM

Zap! Clang! Zip! Wands buzzed, swords clashed, and arrows flew.

"Zennith, keep that arrow straight! Aidryan, your wand needs to be pointed more toward your target! Dagon, don't focus on how you grip your blade more than on your enemy and don't put your guard down!"

It had been almost a month since everyone had cast their first spell. After just a couple weeks, Maylis knew that they were ready. Now they astounded him with their abilities. Their Laminian names had become a part of them and were being used all the time. The names Chris, Mary, and Karl were a thing of the past.

"Okay, let's take a little break from practicing and show off what you've learned. I think you guys are ready to level up!"

Zennith, Aidryan, and Dagon put their gear away in the tents and hurried over to headquarters.

"Aidryan, show us your favorite spell," Maylis suggested.

"All right, I'm going to demonstrate the levitation charm. *Versethy!*"

Immediately, Zennith began to rise up into the air from where he stood.

"I'm afraid of heights!" he yelled, flailing his lanky limbs. To add to his embarrassment, a bird flew by and thought his head was a nice place for a pit stop. "Help! I'm being abused!"

"He sure has a heart of a dragon," Dagon joked.

"That's nothing!" Aidryan pointed at the bird and transformed it into a festive sombrero.

"Nice demonstration, Aidryan. You are quite good at those transformation spells," Maylis complimented a proud Aidryan.

"Aidryan, please change the bird back so it can return to its family and we can continue our training," instructed Maylis. He turned to Zennith. "Okay, Zen, show us what you've got."

"All right. I'm going to make this flaming arrow hit that target over there, forty feet away. *Hasanta!*" As soon as he said it, his metal arrow tip suddenly caught on fire. A burning red flame danced in the light of the afternoon sun. He pulled back and let go. The flaming arrow zipped through the air. *Plunk!* The arrow went through the target and landed in a growing daisy, igniting the flower. He was very proud of himself because this had been a very difficult skill for him to master.

"Well done, well done!" Maylis was very pleased. "Okay, Dagon, let's see what you can do."

"Right." Dagon got up and searched for a big grassy area to focus on. He whipped his hands into the air and closed his eyes gently.

The others expected a giant wave to come crashing into view; instead, they saw something none of them imagined. Dagon had created a huge crystal-clear pool with a diving board, waterslide, and a miniature lazy river. They saw Dagon reclining on a lounge chair and holding a towel. He had sunglasses on and was wearing bright-blue swim shorts.

Zen, Aidryan, and Maylis stood frozen with awe at the wondrous water park their friend just created.

"Just so you know," Dagon called, "you have swimsuits and towels behind you. Last one in has to be one of Erex's minions!"

The next day Maylis called them out for serious business time. "You have now reached the end of your training. I have had a really good time with you here, but your home needs you now." Maylis gave them a disheveled map with a piece missing.

"Is this the map to our home kingdom?" Zen whispered. "Because if our training is done and you're showing us the map, then—oh yeah!"

All three graduates shot out of their seats like cannonballs and started dancing silly. "We did it, we did it! Yeah, yeah, yeah!" they chanted. After about three minutes of nonstop hooraying, they were ready to listen.

"Okay, so this *is* the map to Lamin. But as you can see, it's ripped. Our first priority is to procure the other piece," Maylis said. "But we are in luck because I know where it is. It is located in the Fantasy Museum down on Fifth and Butler. Any questions?"

Aidryan raised her hand. "Are you coming with us?"

"Of course. I can't have you three traipsing around a heavily guarded museum by yourselves and expect you to come out without getting arrested. No offense."

"None taken." She looked over at Zen and Dagon.

Dagon scrunched his face and asked Maylis, "So we're going to break in, steal the other map piece, and bust out like criminals?"

"Not exactly. I have something even cooler in mind."

"Does it involve sleeping gas to make the guards drop to the floor in a heap?" Aidryan asked hopefully.

"Are we going to release a huge bucket of cockroaches so the guards faint and we can take the map piece without getting caught?" That one was from Zennith. He loved bugs.

"Nope," Maylis had a smug look on his face. "We will do something even more fantastic than sleeping gas or cockroach surprises."

All three leaned closer to hear the exciting plan Maylis had prepared to retrieve the missing map piece. Maylis leaned toward them and whispered, "I made arrangements for us to take a tour of the Mystery of Maps room, which is where I believe we will find the missing part of the map."

Not one person was enthusiastic about that arrangement—except, of course, Maylis. He loved learning as much as the next nerd, so going to the Fantasy Museum was his dream come true. He hummed to himself and happily handed out some normal clothes to replace their uniforms. The friends were groaning under their breath as he did that. He ignored them.

"I still don't agree with this. It would be so much more fun to get the map doing something epic or ridiculously hard core," Dagon mumbled, disappointed that he wouldn't even make it in the crime section of the newspaper if they got caught.

"I know, Dag, but let's just do it for Maylis," Zen responded. "He helped us become what we are now. Remember that we had no idea how to use a magic wand. Now we can use them to summon fire, water, and lift unsuspecting people off the ground." He stared down Aidryan while she turned her eyes somewhere else.

"And let's also do it for Lamin's salvation," Aidryan reminded them.

"Yeah, you're absolutely right." Dagon smiled. "We will be doing some awesome things in the future anyway."

Aidryan agreed. "Come on, let's put on our touring clothes."

The trip to the museum was breathtaking because they had never really traveled in the air so fast and so far before. When they arrived at the Fantasy Museum, Maylis told them to practice their old names before entering the building. As soon as they set foot on the museum tiles, their mouths dropped open. The ceiling was painted a rich purple with shimmering sparkles. There was a glass case full of magic wands and werewolf bones to the left of the entrance. Above their heads, hanging from the sparkly purple ceiling was a humongous dragon skeleton—at least that's what the sign said. Its huge fangs pointed down at them. But the most interesting thing they saw was standing on top of the steps right in front of them.

"Hello, welcome to the Fantasy Museum! We are standing in the fairy-tale items collection, and there is so much more to see. My name is Shelli. I will be your tour guide today."

6

THE ESCAPE PLAN

Shelli looked very much like those fancy museum tour guides in the movies. She wore a skirt, dress shirt with an ascot, and perfect hair pulled up in a tight bun. She had very sharp features and long red nails. As she led them through the museum, Dagon had a strong feeling that the missing-map section was near.

Everyone's mood quickly shifted when they entered the Mystery of Maps room. Hundreds upon hundreds of every type of map lined the walls and shelves or were displayed in big glass receptacles. Amazingly, some were exhibited on the ceilings and floors placed under a protective plastic coating.

"Hey, um, Maylis, how are we going to locate a miniature map chunk in all of this?" Zennith gestured with his hands to the mounds and mounds of maps in front of them.

Aidryan stepped forward. "Hello, um, Ms. Shelli, how many maps would you say are in the room right now?" Aidryan held her breath, ready for that significantly high number.

Shelli answered in her sweet high-pitched voice. "Oh, just about one thousand and twenty in this room, but there are plenty more scattered throughout the entire building. Why? Are you interested in a certain famous map like the journey to the Fountain of Youth or maybe the voyage to Mordor because we have them all! Or maybe the map of Lamin, the magical city that rests upon the clouds. It's one of my favorite stories!"

"May we see the ones to Mordor and Lamin please?" Dagon asked swiftly, hoping his obvious red face would fade.

"Of course!" The goddess-like human seemed pleased with her salesmanship. "The Mordor map is over by that window. We don't have the complete Lamin map, but I can show you what we have and give you all the information I can." She led them over to a bulletin board that held many old, musty map specimens that were extremely hard to read. She pointed to one that looked like the words were written in some sort of mythical language.

Maylis cleared his throat. "Too bad the story of Lamin is a myth. Do you know what these symbols mean?"

Everyone turned. He had been so mouselike the entire time, so his friends were a bit startled when they heard his voice. He did his best not to show much emotion for fear he might let his feelings give away their world's entire existence. Maylis's friends got what he was trying to do and did their best to look as though they were clueless on the history of their missing map piece. Luck was with them because Shelli just kept talking, still on topic.

"To answer your question, the letters and symbols on this side appear to be directions and warnings."

Aidryan studied the markings on the paper with curiosity. She recognized some of the letter symbols that Maylis had shown them in the past.

"As you can see, some writing is illegible and a portion of the map is missing so that doesn't help with the translations. Actually, this particular specimen has recently been sold, and Mrs. Farrys will be picking it up today," Shelli said this information casually and without any concern that it was crucial to everything.

"Oh, exciting! When?" Zen asked, trying to be convincing and conversational. He winked at his friends.

"Since it takes a while to process and get papers signed, I believe our guards will be collecting it around 3:30 for a 4:00

p.m. pickup. Always have to be on our toes around here—I mean, like around the clock—all the time!" Shelli informed them. She looked at her watch. "Speaking of time, it looks like our time is up. I hope you enjoyed your tour. Hope to see you again soon!" Shelli called as she hustled out of the map room.

As they walked out, the sun blinded them since they were used to the muted lighting in the museum. It made it extra hard to concentrate on conducting a master plan where sneak attacks and ninja skills would occur. This would be especially tough because the museum had hundreds of statues of mystical beings that Aidryan noticed had tiny cameras in their eyes. On top of everything else, one or two bodyguards stood at attention in every room.

"So, Maylis," Zen asked, "two questions for you. Do you have a plan and are the scribbles on the map legible to you? Also, I'm hungry. Can we storm the castle after we get a hamburger? I can't tear down walls and fight people on an empty stomach. It's just unhealthy. Oh, wait, that was three questions, wasn't it?"

Maylis raised an eyebrow at Zennith. "Well, considering the circumstances and Zennith's stomach, this might be trickier than we thought. My plan will work, but only if it is followed perfectly," Maylis cautioned. He looked at his watch and turned his calm face toward his friends' anxious ones. He motioned for them to move around to the side of the building to discuss the particulars of their raid in private. "I was thinking that we could go back into the museum around 3:20 p.m., just before the map is removed from the wall. We will dress as security guards, specifically the ones who will be covering the transfer of our missing map piece. All we need to make this master plan successful is a little bit of magic. We need the practice. Besides, this is your first real mission, and I want to make it as fun and easy as possible."

Maylis's friends seemed to be very eager about this procedure. They all agreed about not wanting anything to be too tough, mainly because this was their first assignment.

"I was fortunate to see on the museum's section of the map that the markings were indeed of a Laminian nature, and I was able to make out three symbols." Maylis smiled as he saw the eyes light up in front of him. "Can you guess what those words were?" Maylis asked them.

Dagon, Aidryan, and Zennith all looked deep in thought; but they eventually gave up because the suspense was killing them.

"We give up," Dagon said. "What are they?"

"Well, Dagon, the words on that bit of map were proof that we have come to the right place. At the very top of the parchment were three sets of symbols that—"

"Just tell us already! You are giving me huge amounts of anxiety, dude!" Zennith complained.

"Spelled out the 'Map of L,'" Maylis finished. "And yes, we will eat beforehand, Zen. Don't worry. Come on, I'll teach you more about the Laminian language while we grab some food."

After enjoying their meal at Paco's Pastrami and reviewing some ancient Laminian symbols, they were ready to put their strategy into action. Maylis gave them each an outfit and a quick spell for their faces and bodies so that normal people would just see Max, Scott, Bob, and Joan. They were the security guards in charge of transferring the map. Maylis gathered this vital information during a chat with the bouncy salesgirl at the museum's gift shop. He could be very convincing when it came to getting what he wanted. The real Max, Scott, Bob, and Joan were detained in the bathroom after eating the free pastrami samples that were generously left in the employee snack room.

"Ah, there you are. You're late," Liam, the head patrol guard, said as he spotted them through the high-tech surveillance cameras that he was sitting near.

Everyone was extremely cautious, making sure only their special employee badges showed on camera and not their faces. Even though they had a cover, it was still smart to take some precautions. Liam was a tall, kind of chunky man with a neat blond haircut that was slightly raised with hair gel. He wore a navy-blue cap and polo shirt that displayed the word *security* on the high end of his broad back. Obviously, he took his job very seriously. Liam gave Maylis (Max) a cardboard box and an order form.

Aidryan looked around, wondering how an actual museum security guard would act while getting checked in. Then she noticed a sparkling pendant on Liam's neck that was just like the symbol on her black box. She was barely able to contain her excitement. She followed Liam along with Max, Bob, and Scott (Maylis, Dagon, and Zennith) to the Mystery of Maps room. Once there, Liam stuck his immense hands into his small pockets and walked off to attend to other security matters. They all started to relax after that. First stage was done, but sadly there were more difficulties to come.

"Why do you think they're taking all these precautions? It's only a boring museum, right?" Zennith (Scott) asked with a slight trace of concern.

Maylis (Max) answered, "Many rare artifacts are housed in this place. Mrs. Farrys probably gave a *lot* of money to the museum to obtain the map to Lamin. The form that Liam handed me confirmed my suspicions. Turns out, Riley Farrys bought more items than just the map to Lamin. She has a weird obsession, but she gets what she wants because the museum needs money."

"You got all that from an order form?" Dagon remarked.

Maylis sighed, "I wish I did, but that last comment was written word for word on the back."

"Oh, nice eye."

"Thanks, Dag."

It took a while, but they managed to find every item on the list. They purposefully left the Lamin map in its place. Maylis took out a blank piece of paper and recited the copying spell over the museum's part of the map. Aidryan put their copy of the map in a small carrying bag. Dagon put the order form in another. Maylis and Zen carried the items down the hall to the waiting Riley Farrys.

MAP STEALERS

Riley Farrys was a stout middle-aged woman dressed in a velvet coat the color of the sun. A matching tiny hat sat on her small round head. From that tiny hat protruded a single peacock feather. Her face was pretty much expressionless, except for the smirk outlined in reddish-pink lipstick. She stood between two very muscular bodyguards about twenty yards away.

"Hello, ma'am," Maylis greeted her. "Here are the maps and other items you ordered."

"Is this a joke?" she replied. "Where are my regular delivery guards? You *kids* are certainly not Max, Bob, and Scott."

Dagon and the others were unaware that the face-changing spell had worn off and their original faces and bodies had reappeared. Dagon caught his reflection in Mrs. Farrys's shiny brooch. They were in trouble, and they didn't need a fortune-teller to tell them what was going to happen next.

Riley called, "Luke, Peter, seize them immediately! Wait until Liam hears about this. You kids are doomed."

They turned to run. Dagon was beginning to regret this mission and wondering if things could possibly get any worse when Aidryan, who was right behind him, accidentally let their copy of the Lamin map fall out of her bag. Dagon felt a chill run up his back. He heard Farrys yelling to her guards, "Quick! They are trying to get away with *my* map!"

"Zen, Aidryan, Dagon, follow me!" Maylis called to them, barely missing a flying fist from behind. Luckily, the attacker lost his balance, and the friends were able to jump over him and make it out into another hallway. After that dodge, they ended up in the Wax Figure section, out of breath and sweaty in their now baggy clothes. Hearing more fast and angry footsteps tearing down the hall, they swiftly ran and hid behind a curtain by a big sculpture of Merlin, where they tried to regroup and think.

"Guys, are you okay?" Aidryan whispered between heavy breaths.

They all nodded, so she decided to bring up her hunch about the necklace. "Did any of you see the symbol on Liam's pendant? I'm pretty sure it is the same symbol that's on our black boxes!" she said excitedly.

Zennith's face lit up. "I was wondering about that too. I think you're right," he agreed. "Maybe we should tell him who we are and why we're here. He may be able to help us."

"Guys, I think it's time for plan B." Maylis smirked.

"What! Are you crazy?" a frightened Zennith asked, wondering what had gone through Maylis's mind and why *he* had to be the bait. He put on his best protesting face with a side of begging but soon gave up because he remembered that Maylis was extremely stubborn. Mules could not budge him. So long story short, there Zennith stood right in the middle of a hallway lined with wax figures, waiting for two big bodyguards to chase him. But just then, much to Zen's relief, Liam came walking into view, changing the plan a bit.

Now is my chance, Zen thought. *Oh, I really hope I don't screw things up.*

Before Liam could speak, Zennith cornered him and started talking at enormous speed. Sadly, Liam could only make out a few vowels from Zennith's jumbled word play, which made the already-puzzled guard dizzy. Just as Zennith finished telling Liam their story, the friends rushed in to see a horrifying sight. They were expecting the rich lady's two bodyguards, but instead they saw Liam. He had apparently not taken Zen's excuse so well because he looked very put out by the boy's shenanigans. Zennith was being squeezed by the robust security guard and was on the verge of unconsciousness. Then the python-like hug became softer and less aggressive than before. Liam smiled as if finding Zennith was the best thing that ever happened to him, besides becoming a museum guard.

"Quick!" Liam explained. "I have to get you out of here before those rough and tumble guards and their psycho boss catch up!"

The kids didn't have another legit choice at this point, so they thought, *What the heck*, and agreed to follow him. He led them to a maintenance closet and explained that now would be a good time for them to change back into clothes that actually fit them for extra speed. Liam didn't need to tell them twice. When they were back to normal (as normal as this whole situation could be), Liam took them to a hidden exit. One by one they tiptoed through and shut the door ever so softly. They stood in silence for a while as the teens wondered if Liam could be trusted. Maybe he had some answers for them.

Dagon broke the silence in hopes that it would do some good. "Well, let me introduce everyone. This is Maylis, Aidryan, and Zennith." He pointed as he said their names. Dagon wondered if it would be safe to state his name because now that Liam knew what they came for they would be risking everything. Another silence ensued followed by a deep breath. "And my name is Dagon," he added.

Liam's expression quickly changed, which worried Dagon greatly.

"Oh, I thought you looked familiar. Prince of Lamin, is it? Your father contacted me to keep an eye on you and your friends. You look just like him. His Majesty said that you would be coming home soon. He wanted me to make sure you got past your first test." Liam took off his cap and bowed.

Unsure of what to do, Dagon's reflex was to bow back. *Awkward, but not as bad as I thought.* After the little meet and greet, everyone was feeling more loose and free. That made transactions less difficult.

"Do you have the map?" Liam asked.

"Yes, we have a copy of it. The only problem is that we still don't know exactly where we are going," Dagon explained.

"Do you know how to get there, Liam?" Aidryan asked.

"Yes, I do, but I can't help you any more, I'm afraid. Except for keeping you from bodily harm at the museum, your father directly forbade me to assist you because you have to follow your own path. What I *can* do is tell you that there are items you are expected to procure along your journey to Lamin. His Majesty made the rules for a reason, and I suggest we trust him on this one," Liam stated.

The four looked a little bummed but seemed to understand Liam's situation.

Liam motioned with his hand for them to come closer. "You seem like good kids, and I really do wish you the best of luck. At least let me point you in the right direction. I believe that prophecy was something like, 'Four will venture to find an adventure. Three with a tool to help cross the wide pool.' That *wide pool* is the ocean. I believe you should start there." Then he turned and went back into the museum without saying another word.

8

The Wide Pool

"So what's the closest ocean?" Aidryan was just taking out the copy of the map when Maylis plucked it from her grasp. She glared at him.

"I believe that would be the Atlantic." Maylis looked up to meet her gaze. "So finding a train to the beach is next on our agenda."

Fortunately, Zennith spotted a bus across the street that had "Megawatt Rail System" emblazoned on its side. The bus was now departing, so the friends walked over to the small bench and took a seat to wait for the next one. Everything was going well until Dagon opened his mouth.

"Hey, Maylis," he asked, "are there any, you know, sea monsters or cursed ships that we could run into at some point along the way?"

Maylis took in the information like he was thinking about what he could divulge and what would best be kept secret. Meanwhile, glares were being exchanged since Dagon had now made them all ten times more worried.

"I have personally seen no monsters in those waters," Maylis said as the tension relaxed. "Although I wouldn't rule it out." The others gave him a look. Maylis continued, "I have studied the history of Lamin for quite some time and have never heard of *terrible* monsters or curses. Anyway, someone would have mentioned it to me since I am in charge of taking you there." Maylis had an assured look on his serious face.

Maylis lived most of his life in the world of Lamin in a small town far away from the main city. He had never seen the city except once when he was a few months old, which doesn't actually count as seeing it. However, Maylis's mother and father had seen the great city and told him many stories. Besides, if he knew exactly how to get there, he might unwittingly reveal pathways and shortcuts. He didn't want them to follow him like little ducklings. That would suck all the fun out of the adventure. The bus dropped them off at the rail station where they boarded a train headed for the coast. An older couple clutching inner tubes sat in the seat across from them.

When they arrived at the oceanfront, Aidryan called them into a huddle. "Okay, first we lay low until that couple leaves (the couple seemed to be the only people active at this time so they had luck on their sides). Then we go to that dock over there." She pointed behind her. "Finally, we toss in our magical toy boat and speed away from civilization. Any questions?"

Zennith raised his hand. "Can you explain this for simple-minded people?" he asked.

Aidryan did an actual face-palm and took a long deep breath and continued, "Hide, throw boat, get in, bye-bye civilization. Get it now?"

"Yes, I think I get it now."

"Perfect."

They all thought this was a great idea because technically, it was the only viable one they had. Zennith's plan involved hot dogs, ketchup, and mustard, which he would use to squirt the innocent tubing couple in the eyes while the rest of them sped off in the other direction. After his explanation, his friends' faces indicated a million crickets had joined in the strategy. Maylis reached into his tiny magic bag and pulled out diving equipment.

"What's with the scuba outfits?" Dagon chuckled.

"Your father instructed me to bring these items because they are vital to the mission."

Maylis flung the scuba gear at the young heroes, then attempted to tug the pointy toy boat out of the bag.

"He said . . . that . . . you had to . . . travel to Hidden Harbor . . . about ten miles up," Maylis said in between grunts.

Dagon helped him pull the boat out, then scouted for the inner tubing couple. He saw them near the pier facing the other direction, so he threw the toy boat in with a huge splash. There before them floated a small vessel equipped with life jackets, two swivel seats, and an outboard motor. Maylis hopped on and got the engine running while the rest piled on deck, gripping their scuba suits. Zennith couldn't resist wearing his flippers, a rash decision that resulted in a skinned knee. Then they were off and ready for their second adventure. When Dagon inspected the boat, he found out two things: one, there was not that much space on deck and, two, there was even less space below deck. The galley (kitchen) took up half of it, and two beds took up the other half. The tiny storage compartment was barely able to fit the first aid equipment. Dagon, disgusted with the situation, climbed back on the deck to complain, only to find Aidryan and Zennith practicing spells to make turtles and fish dance with each other. Yep, things were pretty normal so far.

"I see your problem," Maylis agreed after listening to Dagon grumble. "It seems this boat was made for two people. With a few changes, we can make it work for four. I'm sure of it." Maylis took stock of their new floating home, then uttered a magic spell that made the boat and everyone in it shake.

"*LAMALASAFFGYUIMA!*"

The heroes' little fishing boat transformed into a fancy yacht. Dagon looked through a window and saw a beautifully redone galley with granite countertops and fancy dishtowels. But the room that Dagon loved most was the planning chamber. It had a wooden placard outside the door and magnificently upholstered couches and embroidered plush pillows. Aidryan and Zennith were also flabbergasted with the remodel and gawked at the entrances to the sleeping areas. Once they saw their beds and comforters, beelining was a complete understatement. They became acquainted with their sheets in a fifth of a second.

After their nap, they enjoyed a relaxing dinner consisting of gourmet peanut butter and jelly sandwiches. Afterward, they changed out of their smelly attire and took nice, long hot showers. They got into their cozy pajamas and bathrobes with matching slippers and met in the lounge. Since it was evening, Maylis dropped anchor to settle in for the night. The companions decided to watch a movie to celebrate their friendship and not dying (yet). When Aidryan won the battle of picking a movie, everyone else was bummed about her choice of *Anne of Green Gables*. Bickering ensued and could be heard many miles away by night fishermen trolling for bottom-feeders. Even though the boys ended up not getting exactly what they wanted, they were all visited by a very peaceful sleep.

Their good night's sleep turned into a rough morning. Dagon and Aidryan heard shouts coming from Maylis's room and came rushing in. Aidryan thought from the horror in his voice that the boat had sprung a leak or the Lamin map was missing. Dagon was thinking the same thing; but as they entered, exhausted and worried, the only thing to fear was Maylis's idea of an emergency. Maylis was on his bed looking at a mirror and screaming with his hands in the air. His black hair had turned a dazzling shade of pink. Zennith was laughing and rolling on the ground, evidently the one to blame for Maylis's predicament. Zen had played this little prank because Maylis made him do the dishes the night before. Zen figured this was *his* boat, so he shouldn't have to do any dirty work.

"Love your new look, Maylis," squeaked Aidryan.

"Very stylish," offered Dagon.

9

THE UNANNOUNCED ENCOUNTER

"Are we there yet?" Aidryan asked.

Maylis sighed, sat down, and took out Dagon's compass and the map pieces they had roughly taped together. "I think we will reach Hidden Harbor soon. We have been instructed to go on a little diving excursion there to find some valuables. Go ahead and suit up." He looked at the compass to pinpoint the exact location of the dive while his friends went to find the scuba gear they stashed in the planning chamber. The masks and suits were color coded, which should have made getting dressed a little less complicated.

Maylis called to them from the upper deck. "The harbor is only one, no, two miles from here!"

Aidryan, Dagon, and Zennith spent the next mile trying to find their arm and leg holes. The mile after that was spent smacking each other with flippers and making rude noises with the snorkels.

"Land ho!" Zennith remarked as they climbed on deck.

Sure enough, there was a small island rising up in front of them. Operation Diving for Treasure was a go.

"Let's drop anchor here and prepare for the dive," Maylis shouted as he climbed down from his lookout position.

"Wouldn't it be easier if you just cast a spell that would allow us to breathe underwater?" Zennith asked.

Maylis thought about this suggestion but told them that having this experience was important. It wasn't a get-in, get-out situation. Before the dive Maylis tried to go over some safety rules but found it difficult to concentrate because his listeners started snickering and pointing at his head. Unbeknownst to him, Zen changed Maylis's hair from pink to green to blue to yellow to orange, then finally back to the "original" fetching pink color, allowing Maylis to finish reviewing the rules in relative peace.

A few minutes of calm were hardly enough to get Dagon, Aidryan, and Zennith back on track and ready for another adventure with possible dangers. Nevertheless, they set off on their excursion with heads full of wonder about the treasure they would find. Upon entering the water, the friends marveled at the beautiful reef below them and were swarmed with many types of colorful fish and sea life. The view was way prettier than on the boat and was a nice change of scenery.

After scouting their surroundings, Maylis motioned for them to move toward the open ocean and away from the reef. After a few minutes of swimming and humming to himself, Maylis looked back and realized that he had not one follower. A bit flustered, Maylis went back toward the coral to have things out with his companions. On the way he tried to come up with some snazzy comebacks and mild threats and didn't notice that he was indeed being followed. Four little fish swam gracefully and ever so quietly above Maylis, avoiding his detection. Back at the coral reef, Aidryan, Zen, and Dagon turned and treaded water when they saw Maylis. Maylis swam up next to them and motioned, "What's wrong?"

The friends' eyes looked huge behind their masks as they watched the four little fish descend.

"How do you do?" said one.

"Hello," said another.

"How are you?" the third one said.

"'Sup?" said the last one.

The first fish that spoke smiled his best fish smile and hovered close to Maylis's mask. "Maylis, how good of you to come by! It *is* you, is it not? Although your hair looks a bit different than I remember—"

"Yes, it's me," Maylis mumbled, too embarrassed to own up to his new look. He glowered at Zen.

The friends were familiar with spells, magic bags, wizards, and even waterfalls that flood backyards; but one thing that never came up in conversation was talking animals, especially English-speaking yellowtails.

Maylis decided not to let his misgivings about his hair affect his outgoing personality. "Well, then, let me introduce everyone. This is Finn, the manager of Fish Valley, and his kinfolk and colleagues, Toby, Felix, and Josh."

"Very nice to make your acquaintance," Finn said politely. "So, Maylis, why did you come to see your old buddies?"

Aidryan finally found her voice. "C-c-could you m-maybe show us around for a bit?" Aidryan took some deep breaths from her tank.

"Of course!" The happy fish chuckled. "Toby, Felix, Josh, show them the giant kelp forest at the bottom of the ravine. I'm going to catch up with my buddy, Maylis."

"Keep up, please!" Toby shouted. He and his colleagues started whispering loudly about how Dagon seemed skittish for a prince.

Dagon decided to keep his distance. He quietly swam a few feet away from his friends and decided to look for a pretty shell or something to bring back to his mom. Thinking about his mom made Dagon feel sad, so to cheer himself up he raced around in the water doing dolphin dives and loops. Then a shiny glint crossed his gaze. He swam over and saw a gold chain intertwined in a clump of seaweed. He examined it and concluded it was Laminian-made.

Dagon wasn't ready to share this treasure yet because it was the only thing he had that reminded him of his dad. He stuffed the sparkling chain into his bag. Just then, Dagon heard his friends' muffled voices and four very small muffled voices calling to him from the top of the reef.

Aidryan was the first to see him and dove straight toward him. Dagon thought maybe he was hallucinating because there was his cousin, floating before him and swishing her bright-purple mermaid's tail. His other friends and fish guides joined them. Instead of two legs kicking, his friends each sported one giant iridescent tail.

"You okay?" Aidryan asked.

"Yeah, yeah, I'm perfectly fine, but I have one small question—whose idea was it to grow fish tails?" Dagon turned to Zen. "It was you, wasn't it? Why am I not surprised? And seashells in your hair! Zen, really, what are you even wearing?" Dagon let out a little laugh.

Zen looked a bit uncomfortable. "I . . . uh . . . I can explain." Zennith's face looked red. "The spell sort of dressed me as if I were a girl. But, I mean, I kind of like this look." Zennith twirled and flipped through the water like a happy little dolphin.

"Our Laminian kinsmen would be so proud to see you in all your finery, Zen." Aidryan laughed.

Maylis took Dagon aside and said, "Yeah, the spell 'accidentally' made Zennith have female accessories." Maylis made air quotes around the word *accidentally*. "The others tried to take off the barrettes and necklace and even tried to change his tail color and makeup with magic but nothing budged an inch." Maylis snickered.

Dagon couldn't help but laugh. He knew that this was payback for Zen's pink hair prank on Maylis earlier. Maylis then confessed to Dagon that he even considered adding glowing hair dye to the mix but decided against it since it could attract attention from menacing sea creatures and not just tiny yellowtail fish.

Maylis's attire consisted of a nice shimmering aquamarine tail. For headgear, he wore a sea-green leaf-and-flower crown. Aidryan also had a flower crown full of beautiful yellow sea flowers. Zen had a Barbie-pink tail to go with all his fancy accessories.

Maylis motioned for Dagon to swim to a clearing in the reef while his friends and guides gathered to watch Dagon's transformation. Maylis lifted his hand in the air, and a big lime-green cloud surrounded Dagon until he was hidden from view. A few moments later, Dagon's new form was revealed. Instead of two legs, he now had one giant lime-green tail. For his new headgear, he wore a circlet encrusted with tiny purple jewels, a crown fit for a prince.

10

THE SIGN OF A KING

"Now that looks like something Lamin would be proud of," Maylis suddenly exclaimed.

"An ancient Laminian cave!" Aidryan gasped. She swam over to inspect the rough opening in the rock and its hand-hewn stone doors. Ancient carvings encircled the doors. "I think this is a secret code," Aidryan said, running her fingers along the etchings. "In that Laminian book I read called *The Sign of a King*, it described how underwater caves like these often have a message or secret code that the seeker needs to decipher in order to enter the cave and find treasure or sudden death—usually death." Aidryan coughed. Maylis had given her some books about the history and culture of Lamin, and she read them from cover to cover. She loved them so much, she even cast a spell on them to make them waterproof so she could read in the shower.

While Aidryan scrounged around in her bag to find the book, Zennith became impatient. He was not in the mood for waiting. With his strong fishtail pushing him forward, he swam behind the cave, hoping to find another way in. He was swimming pretty fast, so he almost missed a suspicious circle carved into one of the outer walls. He swerved over to take a closer look at this circle that was now at eye level. It looked like an old rusty button.

Zennith reached out his scaly merman fingers. *Click!* Zen pushed that magical button without an ounce of hesitation. He eagerly waited to see if it caused an explosion of some kind or a secret passageway to appear leading to infinite amounts of gold and jewels, but no such luck. Soon after feeling disappointed by nothing being blown up, he heard something. *Oohs* and *aahs* came from his flabbergasted friends and the three fish. Although no one was screaming, Zennith decided to check out the situation. He peered around the corner only to be blasted by a blaze of blue light. Its glare reached almost ten feet from the stone doors. He saw his friends instinctively take a few steps back to make room for the heavenly glow.

Apparently, when Zen pushed the button, the letters etched around the doors had taken on the raging blue shine, peeled off the stone, and began floating around randomly. Then they gathered at one very specific spot above the two doors. For a second, they all seemed to be confused, hurrying through and past each other as if to find their place inline. As the confusion died down, the wonder stirred back up as the letters became perfectly visible in the underwater light. The whole entrance lit up like it was decorated for Christmas. Feeling pretty proud of himself, Zennith glided around, nodding and smiling while Aidryan and Maylis decoded the message. His fish friends seemed especially grateful about the discovery and named him the King of Buttons, which puffed Zennith up even more. They explained to him that they had come across the entrance many times in their travels over the years but had never been able to stir the ancient writings into motion.

"I've got it! I decoded the message!" Aidryan shouted happily.

"You mean, *we* got it. *We* decoded the message," Maylis corrected.

Everyone gathered around the still-glowing stone doors to hear what Aidryan and Maylis figured out. They scrambled to get a good view, tripping over their tails in the process. Maylis explained that at first, he didn't understand the words because they were written in Lamin's ancient language that hadn't been spoken in a few thousand years. "So, obviously, it was pretty difficult," Maylis put in, looking very pleased with himself. This turned into a long discussion about Maylis's amazing language skills.

"Hey, you know that cool cave over there?" Aidryan interrupted. "If anyone wants to find out what's inside it, then I suggest you listen up." Aidryan was 300 percent done with boys for a while. She opened her book and began to read from it. "The message says, 'The Sign of a King.' Maylis and I believe this cave was made by our ancestors as a gift for a future prince."

Aidryan looked at Dagon. "We think that *you* are that prince. I've read about these types of things, and it's our best bet."

Maylis jumped in. "We decoded the message and are sure this is where your dad wants us to go. The only problem is that we still don't know how to actually get in."

"Here goes nothing," Dagon sighed. "Hey, guys, check this out."

"*Wow*, where did you find this?" Aidryan gasped as she reached for the necklace. Aidryan pointed to faint markings on the clasp and asked Maylis to translate them.

Moments later, his face lit up, and he did a perfect back flip through the water. "A sign of kings!" Maylis cried. "Now this all makes sense!"

"Excuse me, Maylis, but I still don't understand how that will help us get inside," Zennith asked.

"Don't you see? When someone says, 'The sign of a king,' people are supposed to respond by saying 'A sign of kings' as an honorable reply."

Everyone looked slightly confused, except Aidryan who explained it was sort of like a Laminian version of Marco Polo. If the special saying is spoken, it triggers the response.

"This also means that the necklace came from within the cave itself," Maylis concluded.

"Hold on." Zennith stopped. "I just had a miraculous thought. What if the way to enter this chamber *is* to play Marco Polo?"

His friends looked at him sideways, not quite understanding his proposition. Playing Marco Polo with a rock would be rather ineffective.

"Don't you get it? On the top of this wall, it has the words *the sign of a king*, so we answer it!"

Zennith swam to the exact center of the big stone doors and spoke loud and clear. "A sign of kings!"

There was a rumbling sound, and the ancient doors fell open.

CAN I HAVE CLUE NUMBER TWO, PLEASE?

Although everyone was excited to go inside, Dagon thought it would be prudent to be aware of any possible dangers. He turned to Aidryan.

"Hey, Aidry, could you give us a little info on what to expect here, just for safety reasons?" he asked.

"Good idea," she said as she flipped through her book. A moment later, she stopped on a section, ran her fingers down the page, and read aloud, "Laminian caves and underground chambers may have tunnels and hidden passages that lead to treasure, but are also frequently outfitted with booby traps. Besides avoiding the perilous traps, part of the adventure is avoiding a certain word, which, if spoken loudly, will cause the cavern to collapse in seconds."

A thousand-year-old cave crashing to the ground. *Oopsy!*

As she finished reading, Aidryan saw a footnote with an interesting message:

"BEWARE! All Laminian caves have guardians that protect their bounty and kill if necessary."

Silence.

"Well, what are we waiting for?" Zennith enthused, trying to lift their crumpling spirits. "Let's go find some treasure! There might be mountains of valuables inside, maybe a million precious gems?"

There was absolutely nothing anyone could do to dampen his spirits.

"We would love to come and join you on this adventure," said Finn, "but . . . well, good luck!"

"Yeah, we gotta go," Josh added. "But stay safe and don't die. It's not worth it."

A lengthy, narrow hallway greeted them as the friends proceeded inside. Their eyes could barely see the walls on either side of them as they approached a dimly lit room with a bookcase, desk, and chairs surrounding an antique-looking round table. All the furniture was perfectly intact despite being submerged. They saw no doors other than the ones they came in. They cautiously swam over to inspect every object in the room and pressed against the walls, hoping to find another tunnel or some sort of exit.

"I can't believe there is no other way to get out of this room," Maylis scoffed. "How are we going to examine the rest of the cave?"

Maylis and the others sat down on the chairs, which was logistically difficult, considering their fishy shapes. Zennith propped his chair against the wall, letting his tail dangle. At that moment, they heard a loud grinding noise. The room's entrance sealed up, and the water began to recede. The companions found they had transformed back into their human selves. To everyone's surprise and relief, a doorway revealed itself behind Zennith.

"I'm on a roll today!" Zennith yelled. "Who knew relaxing in a chair was the new technique? My guess is whoever built this thing knew our generation would have a lot less patience."

Everyone laughed.

"Let's just avoid the guardian and get the heck out of here before the water fills up again," Aidryan suggested. "I am *not* ready to be a mermaid again."

The friends ventured down the ornate hallway behind Zen's chair. On the walls were tapestries depicting legends and history about kings, wars, and other interesting topics that Aidryan read about in the Laminian books. After marveling at the design and handiwork of the ancient artisans, Dagon, Aidryan, Zennith, and Maylis came across what looked to be more like a cave and less like a house. Maylis knew at once where they were.

"This is the place where the guardian dwells," Maylis said.

"Looks like it. But be careful, cave guardians are often shape-shifters—and good ones at that," Aidryan added.

"That's very right, girl. Where did you get that information? I wouldn't expect a mere mortal like yourself to know that sort of thing," said a voice other than Dagon, Zen, or Maylis's.

A woman about five feet tall with curly white hair and wrinkled skin stood behind them, smiling ever so slightly. Then she vanished as suddenly as she had appeared. This was a bit alarming for the companions. After all, if you know there's a huge spider in your bedroom, you prefer to know where it is.

"That is kind of what I meant about being dangerously good shape-shifters." Aidryan gasped.

Out of nowhere, the friends realized that they still were not alone *and* that the cave walls were very echoey.

"I know for what you are searching!" the old voice croaked.

"Oh, great! She's back again," Zennith groaned. "We really don't have time for this. But since I am on, like, the biggest roll ever right now, things *could* go perfectly."

"I see you are a group who was fortunate enough to have cracked the code and ventured within these mysterious walls." She suddenly appeared a foot in front of them holding a torch. "Since you are here, I may as well tell you your future."

Aidryan explained to the others that allowing the guardian to tell their future was unusual and stressed that it may not end well. Maylis was the first to speak to Granny.

"Um, you *are* the cave guardian, right?" Maylis asked.

She whisked herself away to a nearby rock balcony before answering him. "I have been dwelling here for many, many years and feel like I have lost my purpose. But you are here now, and it's time to hear your future!" She looked at them with big wise eyes and spoke again. "Lamin is in trouble! A dark wizard is preparing for his big return—"

"Why are you telling us this?" Dagon had to ask.

The Laminian lady smiled and looked at each of them in the eyes, answering them a little less harshly this time. "Like I have said, I have lost my purpose. From what I understand, you and your entourage are on a quest to find Lamin. I am telling you this, my prince, because I fear for the safety of Lamin, my home. I do not want it and all of its inhabitants to be destroyed by a maniac."

"Okay, how come you know so much?" Zennith blew up.

"Well, I am a pretty wise old being." The grandma guardian laughed. She leaned close to Zennith's ear and whispered softly, "Just so you know for future reference, every villain, fortune-teller, wizard, and monster always knows the details because we really like to gossip." She paused for a while, giving Aidryan and the others time to respond.

"Maylis, if she knows—" Aidryan stopped herself just in time. She just could not ask it, but the question still floated in her head. *If she knows all the answers, why do we have to deal with all these obstacles on our journey to Lamin? Why can't she just help us fly in for the rescue?*

"Because, my dear, all this is an important part of the journey you must take. You must let the truth fall in front of you in a different way than you're used to or it could be too late."

Aidryan glanced over at Maylis, whose expression was a little shaken. "Was that the question you were about to ask me?" Maylis inquired.

Aidryan nodded and was concerned with the fact that she was incredibly easy to read. The guardian looked over at her and cracked a slight smile.

"How about I read you the prophecy once again and maybe, just maybe, you kids will get a bit more out of it and fill in some pieces along the way." She led them away from the entrance where they stood and down an old tattered staircase to what looked like a large gazebo. They came to the center where an immense book sat in the middle of a circular table, looking ready to show off all the knowledge it contained. Still, it was rather surprising when the book rustled and came to life.

"Well, that's something you don't see any day!" Zennith exclaimed.

"It's *every* day, Zen," Dagon corrected. "Actually, you really don't see anything like that in your life. Not every week or every month—never in your life!"

Zennith shrugged. "I am still so on fire today, it's not even funny anymore."

"It was never funny," Aidryan mumbled.

The book and guardian ignored them both.

"OMG, how rude! I totally forgot to introduce myself," the book said.

"It's a little weird that it knows the term *OMG*," Maylis whispered to Zen.

"Or that it can talk without lips," Zennith whispered back.

"Touché," Maylis responded.

The grandma guardian picked up the book. "My name is Sarina, Guardian of the Cave of Gold." As soon as she lifted up the magic book, she looked much younger. No more wrinkles or frizzy unkempt hair. The shape-shifter had now transformed into a pretty middle-aged woman. "This lovely tome is Viran," she added.

"*Bonjour! Je m'appelle* Viran. *Comment tu t'appelle?*"

"You have to excuse Viran," Sarina told the awestruck travelers. "He speaks fluent French and . . . well, every language, in fact. Viran has been my constant companion during this lonely time."

The friends just rolled with the idea of a talking book because things like that were getting surprisingly common. Sarina opened her multilingual companion and read the prophecy aloud.

> *Four will venture to find an adventure.*
> *Three with a tool to help cross the wide pool.*
> *One will pursue a talent hid,*
> *While another gets caught in a pyramid.*
> *One finds riches in the mountain pass,*
> *While another finds the most valuable treasure at last.*

12

THE NEXT CHAPTER

As Sarina read the prophecy a second time, everything started to fall into place.

Four will venture to find an adventure. That, obviously, was Maylis, Dagon, Zennith, and Aidryan.

Three with a tool to help cross the wide pool. Again, obviously, the tools were Dagon's compass, Zennith's boat, and Maylis's magic bag.

Since they had succeeded with the first two lines, they suspected that completing the next line was not far behind.

The guardian walked around the young heroes. "One will pursue a talent hid," she said quietly. She looked around at the blank stares of her listeners. Evidently, they didn't quite understand what that meant. "Let me give you a hint." The now-sweetened voice of the guardian said, "The next four lines will describe each person's fate."

Quickly, Dagon spoke up. "Wait, why are you telling us all of this? Aren't we supposed to figure everything out by ourselves?"

She laughed slightly, then answered again very sweetly. "I'm just guiding you, my dears. Since I took some of your time away from you, it is the least I can do. Plus, you are my prince. I know you are quite skeptical about this whole thing." She turned to her book friend, and it nodded. It seemed like Viran knew what to do because at that moment he sighed and copied himself, splitting into four mini notebooks. Sarina reached for one of the mini books and explained to the teenagers, "These are like cell phones of the ancient people. With this pen, you simply write a message on any blank page. I'm giving them to you so you can always talk to me no matter where you are in the world. Write me if you are in trouble or just need to talk." Sarina smiled.

"*Wow*, that's really nice of you," Aidryan said. "But I was just wondering if you could explain something. In the books about Laminian folklore, guardians were sometimes depicted as being deceiving and their gifts sometimes lured visitors into traps."

As soon as she questioned Sarina's integrity, she got accusing looks from her friends that screamed, "OMG, are you serious right now?" and "Like, she is *way* more powerful than us!" and "We are so doomed!"

Sarina sighed, and her face fell a bit. She explained that cave guardians were chosen by whoever found the cave first. That person had to pick from the available, unassigned guardians. Each guardian had his or her own personality: mean, sad, vengeful, deceitful, and good. "You can imagine what sort of guardians people were tempted to pick," Sarina said. "Once picked, the guardian stayed in their assigned cave until they died or someone else took their place. A few years ago, however, the king said that since the caves were becoming obsolete, I was to allow visitors to pass through without a struggle. I am merely the caretaker."

The companions stood in silence for a while, not breathing a word but contemplating what to do in their heads. Suddenly, Dagon's face lit up. "Hey, guys! Can't she just come with us?"

As soon as Sarina heard that, her face beamed brightly. "I should leave you to accomplish this quest on your own, but the truth is, I would love to accompany you. Maybe you could just drop me off at the nearest town," she said.

They agreed, although an extra person would have been a nice thing to have aboard.

"Absolutely," agreed Dagon.

"Oh, you're a dear!" Sarina hugged all of them tightly before rushing around and trying to put a decent suitcase together.

"Okay, let's be off!" Maylis called. He and the others prepared to climb back up the long, twisty stairs when they heard a call from down below.

"Where are you crazy kids going? There is a perfectly good exit down here." Sarina laughed.

The friends shrugged their shoulders and pushed past each other to get down. Dagon was very happy to finally get out of here but also kind of sad because Sarina was leaving them. They finally found someone who was crazier than they were, so he wanted to cherish this moment. She would have been a pretty good secret weapon to have on board. Sarina grabbed a few other belongings, while Viran and the mini books stayed with the teens.

"This tunnel leads to the top, but we will have to swim through a bit of water. I suggest that we turn into those fishy things again and swim on out," Sarina said.

In a few seconds Maylis began transforming them back into ridiculous mermaids, but there was one minor problem. He gave them tails to match their hilarious flower crowns, but this time, their tails were not attached to their bodies and were thrashing wildly twenty feet away. Now I don't know what kind of weird things you've seen before, but surely nothing could compare to four teenagers in flower crowns and a middle-aged woman flailing all around trying to grab speeding mermaids' tails while bumping into each other. It would definitely have made it on *Lamin Kingdom's Funniest Videos* if someone caught this scene on camera.

"There's the exit!" Sarina yelled as soon as all the tails attached to their person. "Follow me!"

After about ten minutes of shuffling and pushing with some shouts of "*Ow!*" and "*Really, Zen?*" five mermaids shot toward the surface to find their boat, which they hoped was still in one piece. Aidryan figured some weird stuff would happen on their dive, but she didn't think it would be anything close to the craziness of the museum heist. Of course, all that changed when she met fish that could carry on a conversation, investigated magic underwater caves, became acquainted with Grandma Guardian, and heard a book speak French. They swam around for a while, trying to locate their boat.

Zen called out to his friends from a distance, "Guys, look! I found it!"

"I really hope he doesn't say it again," Aidryan mumbled.

"I am *so* on fire!" Zen yelled.

"Darn it!"

Aboard the yacht, everyone reclined on lounge chairs because the fishtail spell had not completely worn off yet. It had been quite a challenge to get everyone on deck since no one could walk. After everyone was human again, the boat ride became enjoyable. Zen started a game of ping-pong with Dagon that Dagon regretted every time Zen scored, which was often. Sarina told Aidryan everything about their magical home world, from its unique animals to huge castles, including the one Dagon was born in and where his dad now waited for him. Even though Sarina had been stuck in the cave for eons, every so often, each guardian would go back to Lamin, hang out with the king, and enjoy a huge feast. Then they'd return to their cave to continue their work.

Sarina sighed, "The last time I was home was when Dagon was a year old. I haven't had much interest in going back until now." She beamed at Dagon just as he missed the ping-pong ball yet again. Viran was busy telling Maylis each language he knew and even taught him some words. Maylis had always wanted to learn another language, and now he could say that he had learned from a book. Zen had won ten games in a row, and Dagon was seriously thinking about using his water powers to subdue him somehow. Before he had a chance to, Sarina called them all over to discuss something.

"Like I said, the next four parts of the prophecy focus on one person. Zen, I believe the next one concerns you. You will need to figure out the next three on your own. That's part of the fun. Now my stop is coming up in just a little bit, and I need some help getting everything onto the dock. Oh, and, Dagon, would you say hello to your father for me?" She scurried around the ship with Viran under her arm, grabbing things that she thought she needed and a few mementos as well. The yacht gently bumped the dock. Sarina disembarked with Viran in hand, waving as she walked down the pier.

As evening came the friends gathered around the maple wood table in the planning chamber. The sky seemed to reflect their moods as a gust of wind swayed the boat. None of them thought their life would be the same since Sarina had gone. Her sunny personality brought up their spirits, and they knew they were lucky to have found her. They also knew obtaining information would be way harder in the future. To keep their minds off it, they decided to search the now very improved boat for anything that might be useful to them on their journey.

Aidryan combed the whole boat, and after coming up empty, she decided that she deserved a much-needed swim. Maylis had felt it necessary to add a six-foot-deep pool and hot tub on the roof even when they were surrounded by water. Typical Maylis. Aidryan grabbed a towel and climbed the regal steps to the top where the cloudy sky looked on her as she reclined in one of the lounge chairs. As soon as she put her head down, she realized that her life had never been relaxing. Aidryan's mind drifted to her half sister from her father's first marriage. Skye was about eleven years old when Aidryan was born. She always seemed to have everything: great clothes, perfect manners, and loyal friends. Skye was a people magnet, and everyone adored her. But when she was eighteen, she got mixed up with the wrong crowd, convicted of a felony, and sentenced to five years in prison. That was eight years ago. Aidryan and her family hadn't heard from her since. She hoped that maybe one day Skye would surprise them and say she was back for good but that didn't seem very plausible to Aidryan right now. Still, one good thing did come from that horrible incident. Her family moved soon after to live closer to her aunt. It was then that she met Dagon for the first time. She had been really excited to meet her long-lost cousin at last. At first she was unsure about him, but as she got to know him, that feeling went away and they became great friends.

She smiled, remembering how he would always compliment her outfits even when she knew she looked horrible. Then Aidryan thought about when she started her new school. It was not as smooth a transition as she had hoped. Bullies began to pop up out of nowhere. For a while the only joy she felt at school was when Dagon was around. She never really thanked him for making her feel included and for laughing at her terrible jokes. Aidryan ventured into the pool. She sighed, ducked her head underwater, and dove down to skim the bottom. She pretended she was eight years old again and imagined she was a fearsome shark that no one could take anything from or mess with. She twisted and jumped and dove over and over again until the sadness quieted. She surfaced and caught her breath. Aidryan figured since no one was around it would be a good time to practice some magic. She concentrated on the waterslide a few feet away. Suddenly, water started flowing down it like a waterfall. She smiled and swam under it, singing a Laminian song Sarina taught her.

Walk the bridge over evil, through the lake of mercy,
Under the pain of valor, you will find your courage.
Hmm, hmm, hmm!

*Long has your heart desired adventure, brave and
true.
Give your all and never stop, and it will come to
you.
La dee dum, la dee dum!*

"*Wow*, that was really pretty! I didn't know you had a voice like
that."

Aidryan was taken off guard and jumped so high, she suspended herself five feet in the air, hovering with a flying spell.
Something like that usually happened when she felt danger. It was
a reflex she couldn't control.

Dagon tried not to laugh and sat down on a pool chair.

"*Um*, what are you doing here? I thought you were with
Maylis and Zen?" Aidryan asked as she lowered herself down to
the deck and fixed her hair.

"I was, but I heard something up here. You know me, I just
had to investigate."

"Right."

"Well, sorry to bust in on you like this, but the guys and I
were hoping to have a pool party up here. We were just thinking
that since everyone was a little down lately . . " Dagon trailed off.
"We would let you stay of course."

Aidryan actually thought it would be a great way to lift everyone's spirits. It would probably be the last carefree time they'd have
in a while. "Yes, I think that's a good idea," Aidryan agreed.

"*Woo-hoo!*" Dagon yelled as Zen and Maylis jumped on deck,
already in their swimming trunks.

Dagon slapped on his goggles, threw off his shirt, and jumped
in, followed by Zen and Maylis. Aidryan shrugged and headed for
the high diving board. She put out her hand, and her goggles came
flying to her, whipping around a corner and almost hitting Maylis
in the process. She had to admit that she had some style when it
came to summoning objects. She concentrated on the water below

and prepared to do her famous flip dive to start the party off. She set her mark and jumped, flipped twice, and spun around into a perfect ball that made a huge splash and completely covered Zen and Maylis. The party had begun.

The next hour was spent doing party games and contests like who could make the biggest splash (Aidryan was the reigning champ) or who could tell the best story by ending it with a specific jump into the pool (Zennith won that one, of course). Aidryan found herself happy and laughing throughout the whole party, which meant so much to her. She realized these kids were more than just her cousin and friends. They were family. She intended to keep it that way. Just then, Aidryan's musings were cut short when a water balloon came flying straight for them.

"Duck!" Zen motioned to his friends. He said it just in time for them to grasp the situation and act quickly. The balloon missed its target (Zen's head) and hit the side of the boat with a splash. A second vessel about the same size as their own bobbed in the water next to them.

13

THE WATER BALLOON FIGHT

Teenagers. Not two, not five, but fifteen older teenagers with water balloons in each hand were glaring at them from the deck of their boat. Dagon, Aidryan, and Zennith peered over the railing to get a closer look. They could tell from the older kids' expressions that serious water balloon throwing was imminent. Maylis, on the other hand, was not on the same page. He had never been in a water balloon fight and was unaware of the consequences of aggravating people who were fully loaded and ready to fire. He cleared his throat to talk to their new visitors.

"Hello, friends! What a beautiful day it is." Maylis looked at them, expecting the same positivity back, like "Oh yes, fine. Fine indeed" or "Ah, you are right, my good man!"

The older kids gathered at one end, snickering at how helpless the younger kids were. Of course, they were unaware of the fact that each one of those smaller children could turn them into insects or capsize their precious boat and watch them tumble off screaming. Meanwhile, the kids pulled Maylis down behind the wooden railing and tried to convince him that these people were not there for pleasant conversation and afternoon tea. During this intervention, Dagon gulped as he recognized Ty Gunnar, a football star from school that was always picking on him. He motioned to Aidryan that Ty was there, and she responded by pointing to another teen. Makayla Martin had never been a huge fan of Aidryan's either.

Maylis was finally getting the hint and racked his brain for strategies. After a few moments of head-scratching, he came up with something and quickly told his friends about it. They all thought Maylis should be punched in the face. Aidryan was the first to actually express that thought.

"Are you crazy?" she yelled.

Maylis explained his plan in more detail and was eventually able to get them all on board. Then he went off in a corner to "take care of something."

Zennith was pretty pumped about the idea and decided to share his thoughts with their adversaries. "I am on fire today, so watch out!"

After getting some menacing looks in return, Zennith and his companions prepared for battle.

Ty was the first to shatter the silence. "Well, what do you know! Looks like our toddler friends have stolen a boat and have come to challenge us guys to a fight."

"*Um*, guys?" said one of the female balloon-wielding teens.

"Right. You've come to challenge the *big people*!" Ty corrected. Ty wasn't particularly gifted with intellectual smarts.

Makayla gave Aidryan a dirty look but kept her remarks to herself. It was now time to put the plan into action.

Maylis stepped forward and looked at Ty. "We accept your challenge. Whoever wins gets to keep the other team's vessel. The losing team will have to paddle in an inflatable life raft to the nearest dock." Maylis pointed to a rather small pre-inflated boat. "This floatation device can fit fifteen people as long as you choose the right place to sit." He chuckled.

"Okay, deal!" Ty said smugly. "But on one condition, there will be no rules!"

"Spoken like a true—" Aidryan began but stopped herself when she saw Maylis's warning glare.

The older teenagers huddled to plan their strategy. The heroes discussed theirs in a very low whisper so no one could listen in.

"Remember, we have access to an unlimited number of water balloons, thanks to my trusty magic bag." Maylis patted it affectionately. "We all know what to do. No harm will come to anyone unless someone ticks me off." Maylis grinned.

"READY, SET, GO!" Ty yelled.

Bam! A balloon exploded against a wall right above Dagon's shoulder, splashing water on him. "I guess the game has started," he concluded as he aimed one at Ty's head. He called it "returning the favor."

Aidryan cannoned one toward Makayla's leg in an attempt to make her fall, but at the last possible moment Makayla turned slightly, so it missed its target and hit another teenager squarely on the nose at full Aidryan-powered speed. Purple pieces of balloon were splattered everywhere. Zennith, who was still on fire, was whipping water balloons left and right. His hands were like fully automatic machine guns, rapidly firing at anything that moved. Surprised by this onslaught, the older teens ran a little faster and got a little more nervous. Zennith made it clear that they were in his line of fire. He even took it upon himself to remind them again that he was on fire and boasted about everything that he had accomplished that week. Of course, that was relatively difficult because 98 percent of what he had done was magic related, so the sentences were just a confusing jumble. This made every single person, including his friends, want to aim at him directly.

"Okay, Fireball. I've had enough of your sass!" Ty screamed. "I'm the only one that gets to be arrogant around here!"

At that moment eighteen kids turned their faces up in awe. A twelve-foot-wide water balloon hovered above Ty and his comrades under the control of Maylis of Lamin. "Looks like you missed one," he said.

14

ZEN IS STILL ON FIRE

The opposing teens' first reaction after seeing the humongous water bomb was to scream and run around. That didn't really work out for them because by this time the balloon had grown eyes, arms, legs, and a working mouth. When Maylis let go and the balloon fell, it split into twenty smaller balloons with the same features. More fruitless screaming and running ensued aboard the other boat. The heroes calmly observed the chaos from the safety of their deck, but when the balloons tried to make conversation with the older teens, they totally lost it. Maylis almost fell off the boat from laughing so hard. He was curled up like a pill bug, clutching his aching sides. The rest of the companions nearly joined him because of the priceless reactions they saw from the school bullies. Apparently, Ty and Makayla forgot to keep their cool and were racing across the yacht to avoid answering the questions of the talking balloons.

You could hear Makayla in the distance screaming at one pesky balloon that would not leave her alone. "No, I don't know what Lamin is! I really don't care about this prince guy, and I don't even know why I am still talking to you!" she shrieked.

Once Maylis calmed down a bit, his friends gathered around him. Dagon asked, "So we all expected the huge balloon

68

at the end, but how on earth did you make it split and come alive like that?"

"Do you remember the 'cell phone' books that Sarina gave us that we could use to write messages to her?" Maylis asked. "Turns out, we can FaceTime with her on them too."

The others looked at him strangely but let him continue with his story about how he asked the guardian for help. "She also sent a message to you guys." Maylis cleared his throat and stated the message loud and clear, which was a little difficult because of all the screaming on the other boat, but somehow he managed to get the point across.

"She hopes to see everyone in Lamin very soon, and she wishes us the best of luck on our journey."

Aidryan felt sad suddenly but now was definitely not the time to sit down and cry about it. There was work to be done. "Dagon, I know I don't need to remind you, but we are on a time-tight mission right now." She paused and turned to Maylis. "Maylis, I know you are having lots of fun with this—we all are—but we have to finish it up and get these people on their way so we can go on ours."

Maylis sighed, "Fine. I'll send the balloons away, but it will make me very sad. They understand me!" Maylis grabbed one of the plump magical creatures and squeezed it so hard, its arms and legs swelled from the pressure.

Meanwhile Aidryan was still focused on the task at hand. "Zen?"

"Yeah?"

"Are you on fire?"

"*Um*, no? I have never been on fire in my—oh! Yes, of course, I am on fire! I am bursting with flames!"

"I thought so, since you've brought that up frequently since we set out on this quest."

"True. What do you want me to do?" Zennith asked curiously.

Aidryan silently whispered the plan to him while Dagon and Maylis were off playing dodgeball with the chatty flying balloons.

"Oh, boy! That is sooo good. *Hah!* They will never see that coming," Zen squealed.

Once Dagon and Maylis finished building a barricade to shield themselves from the friendly inflatable missiles, they listened to Aidryan's plan. They showed their approval by rubbing their hands together like evil villains. Aidryan ran off to put her plan into action while the boys diverted their opponents. When she reached the pool area, she focused on one of the white lounge chairs, closed her eyes, and concentrated. Her hands reached out, and colorful blasts of power shot out of her fingertips and enveloped the chair.

A minute later, something large cast a shadow over both boats. Everyone, including the talkative balloon creatures, stopped what they were doing and looked up. A dove-white winged horse glided ten feet above them.

15

AN INTERRUPTING KNOW-IT-ALL

Ty, Makayla, and the rest of their oppressive gang had dealt with enough strange situations for one day. Their motor started, and they zoomed far, far away from the talking balloon creatures and mutant chair-horses. The kids could hear Ty's voice in the distance. "We are not finished here! We will be back! I bet my life we will be back!"

Aidryan sighed and broke the silence. "Well, that was—"

"Interesting," Dagon finished.

Aidryan nodded slowly in agreement. Now they all turned to face the horse that had alighted on the deck. Aidryan was so close to it, she could see up the beast's nostrils.

"Hi," Zen tried.

The winged chair-horse made its way past Aidryan and stepped between Dagon and Maylis so that it was standing right in front of Zennith. The horse sniffed Zen's hair. Zen tried as best he could not to flinch. He needed to show his companions that he was still on fire and not afraid of a flying deck chair. He gulped as he held out his slightly shaking arms toward the creature and closed his eyes in anticipation. *Be brave,* he thought. He was half expecting his hands to be bitten clean off, but what a pleasant surprise! His arms only felt wet. It wasn't like blood-dripping wet,

more like slobber wet. Not only that but a pulse ran up his fingers, through his arm, and finally to his heart. Right then and there Zennith had a feeling this mysterious horse was not going to harm any of them. It may even play a key role in their crazy journey. He swung his wet arms around the creature and hugged it real tight. His friends laughed as the horse whinnied.

"Well, he's definitely not dangerous." Aidryan grinned. "We should name him. Is it a *him*?"

Aidryan and Dagon both looked at Zennith. Zen sighed when he realized what his friends were asking him to do. After checking, Zen got up and took a deep breath for dramatic effect as if he were a game show host and his friends were anxious contestants. "It's a—"

"Pegasus?" Maylis interjected. He obviously had not been paying too much attention to the situation in front of him.

"Well, yes, I think that was fairly obvious." Zen gave him a sarcastic hello-I'm-not-finished-my-sentence-bro look. Maylis inched back, embarrassed about his outburst. Zennith took that as a sign that he could continue without any more rude interruptions. "It's a girl," he finished.

Aidryan cheered loudly. She was glad it was a girl solely because she was the only girl on the boat since Sarina was gone, and she'd had enough "boy" for a while. "So what should we name *her*?"

Silence. Shuffling feet. Awkward glances. The three companions may have stolen a map dressed as security guards, hung out with talking fish, become mermaids, befriended an ancient guardian, met a talking book, and won a magic water balloon fight all in under a week. But none of that compared to the complexity of naming a chair-horse thingy a cool but powerful, easy-to-say girl's name. Poor Maylis couldn't concentrate on names at the moment. He was thinking of an appropriate way to apologize to Zennith for interrupting him and ruining his big moment. He didn't want to upset *any* of the heroes. After all, once the quest was over he was hoping they would let him stay at the castle. Maylis was so distracted with his thoughts he didn't notice a shadow moving behind one of the ship's doors.

Ryan, one of the older teens from the water balloon fight, stowed away on the heroes' yacht and now peered from behind the door, watching Maylis closely. His job was to spy on the little freaks, see what they were up to, and report his findings back to Ty. Ryan probably wouldn't have taken the job if it weren't for the $8.95 a day Ty had promised him. Ryan slinked away from behind the door and moved to Dagon's cabin to look through his things. A book fell out of one of Dagon's bags. It was all about Lamin, what food was popular there, modern clothing style, etc. Ryan opened the book and started reading.

Back on the deck, Dagon, Zennith, and Aidryan were still debating suitable names for their equine companion while the pegasus made herself comfortable on a beach towel. The kids started throwing names around, but none of them seemed to be making the cut until Zennith (still on fire) came up with a really unique, rare, and beautiful one.

"I've got it!" he exclaimed. "We should name her—"

"Rarity!" Maylis suddenly appeared with a golden ring between his fingers and a big smile on his face.

Everyone looked at him in shock. Even the pegasus looked surprised. Zennith marched over to where Maylis stood. Maylis's face darkened once he realized what he had just done—again. Zennith took the ring from Maylis's sticky fingers and smacked him lightly on the head.

16

THE RING

"*Uhhh!*" Was about all Maylis could mutter.

Zennith looked straight into Maylis's eyes. "Where did you find this?" Zen shoved the ring in his face.

Maylis answered in a proud, strong voice, "I just happened to come across it while cleaning your room this morning. I found it on the windowsill and saw the name 'Rarity' engraved on it. It's been in my pocket ever since."

Dagon suppressed laughter but wished he hadn't because of the ridiculous sound that came from his mouth. Aidryan looked at him with one of those "Really, Dagon?" expressions.

Maylis now asked what he hoped were thoughtful questions to try to switch the focus back on Zennith. "How did the ring come to be in your possession? Do you know someone who has that name?" After he said that, he realized his hopefully helpful questions had fallen flat.

Zennith quickly coughed. Everyone, including Maylis, felt a little uneasy. Maylis then opened his mouth to change the subject again, but Zennith wanted to ask his own question. "So what do you know about it, Maily?"

Maylis found it difficult to explain something to someone who had just called him Maily, but he guessed it was some sort of twisted payback for ruining (more than once) Zen's shining moments.

"In the short time I've spent with it," he began, "it's made an occasional buzzing sound. I think it may have made a cup fall from a table. At least that happened while I was going through—never mind. But I could've just been seeing things because I am presently on medicine."

Dagon cut him off. "*Uh*, Maylis, thanks for telling us your incredible story, but I think you should let Zennith talk right now. Right, Zen? Zen?"

Zennith was staring at the ring. It brought back so many memories. Dagon jabbed him in the back. Zen snapped out of his trance and got the memo. "*Ah*, right!" He seemed a little unwilling to continue the conversation with his friends. It was as if his past life had just bitten him on the arm.

It started to rain. Everyone sensed Zen's mood had something to do with the downpour. A few times during training, Zennith would accidentally make it sprinkle when he was angry for missing a shot or stuck on a certain spell. This, however, was the first time it rained because of sadness. The friends hunkered down together under a beach towel to avoid the rain while they listened to Zennith's story.

Ryan was still reading Dagon's book and didn't know whether to believe it or not. He was still debating if he would even tell Ty. He knew that trusting a strange book would be foolish and he would need a little more proof than that. (Unfortunately, he missed Aidryan's chair-horse show. Bummer!) Ryan mulled over his options. Would exposing their true identities be a good thing for him? Would he get a reward? His pocket vibrated, interrupting his thoughts.

"Hey, dude!" Ty said. "Find anything yet?"

KARL'S STORY

Her name was Rarity. Although they had been only ten, he still remembered her like it was a trip up Mount Everest. It was kind of strange how they met.

Karl Weston walked up the short steps to his new elementary school. As soon as his feet touched the linoleum, he knew he had made a huge, really noticeable mistake. Uniform Disaster Day had begun. The other students sported white shirts; he had a loud printed shirt. The kids wore khakis; Karl wore jeans. On top of that, everyone had black dress shoes. And Karl? Karl had scuffed sneakers. He hoped the kids talking to one another wouldn't notice the new, slightly tall, confused human being wandering the halls. To his disappointment, everyone, including some teachers, stared at him. He stopped, waiting for the world to reverse itself so he could finally be free from embarrassment. Then they swarmed him with questions.

"Are you the new kid?" one asked.

"You know you have to wear a uniform, right?" asked someone else.

"What's with the bed head?" sneered another.

From what Karl concluded, not much fun was had around here. Karl guessed that this school was for children that grew up in families that only cared about good grades and how many hours you studied. Although Karl hadn't experienced many situations like this, he could tell from their faces they accepted that this was what life was about and "fun" was only used as a reward for hard work. Where Karl used to go, kids ran down hallways and chased each other with pencils and pointy art projects instead of reviewing vocabulary cards for the ten thousandth time.

Karl had always been a little shy, and new people were hard for him to talk to. He pushed his way gently but firmly out of the "Let's crowd around the shy new kid" circle and headed to homeroom. Since most of his classmates were still at their lockers gossiping and doing last-minute flashcard reviews, which he thought was absurd, it was a nearly empty classroom, except for a smiling teacher who gestured him to a closet. Not to put duct tape over his mouth and abduct him, but only to offer him an extra uniform and black shoes. She grabbed the clothes and motioned to the classroom bathroom. No words were exchanged to complete this transaction.

Karl had never had the pleasure of having a classroom bathroom at his disposal like that. He smiled for the first time since setting foot in this school, gratefully took the clothes from the teacher, and headed inside to change. His fellow classmates arrived just in time to see Karl sitting in the front row of desks. His new uniform seemed to glow with radiance, and he had even combed his hair to add some extra pizzazz to his look. All the other kids could do was stand completely still with their mouths wide open. He ignored their gaping faces until they all unfroze and sat down at their desks, completely silent. If this was how they were going to play, Karl decided to take control and show that he belonged. He stood up, smiled with an A-plus attitude and said, "Good morning, fellow students! I'm new, and can I just say how wonderful it is to be here? My name is Karl Weston, and I am delighted to be part of your class!"

It looked like his streak of confidence worked. He sat down with a little smirk. He could see his new teacher smiling at him from behind her computer. Karl knew he had won the students' respect but decided to take some precautions if he was going to remain untouchable. As he was thinking about this, he noticed some kids behind him were whispering to one another. What happened within the five minutes they had bombarded him with questions to the time he introduced himself, utterly confident with combed hair? It almost seemed that he were two different people playing two different roles. A doppelganger maybe? The students' conversations stopped when Karl turned to look at them. After about thirty awkward seconds the teacher left her desk, still in a joyful mood, and practically skipped to the Smart Board. Class had begun.

Zennith paused for a bit at this part of his story because he noticed that his friends were completely silent. He assumed one of two things: one, he could have a piece of food in his teeth, or two, he could actually be a good storyteller. He continued his story in hopes of the second scenario.

"Hello and good morning, everyone! My name is Miss James. I see you have met the newest addition to our school, Karl Weston." She beamed. "Thank you for the introduction, Karl."

Karl glowed with pride at the last sentence. At this point, however, he was slightly confused as to why this teacher even taught here. Everyone else at this school seemed to have some issue with new people, except her. It was a nice change. He thought this might actually be the year when he could feel like someone special. Throughout the entire day, Karl was able to focus, speak loudly and clearly, read in front of the class, and raise his hand so much his shoulder hurt. Of course, he was very excited for lunch. Karl's first day had been a breeze. He strode confidently down the hall, out of school, and toward the buses. Then he stopped right then and there. Out of the corner of his eye, he thought he saw the sun move abnormally fast.

Now, Karl was one of those kids who liked to let things be and allow nature to handle all the elements. He wasn't naturally motivated to investigate when something didn't seem right. If something out of the ordinary did happen, he would just let someone else deal with it. But for some reason, his brain chose a different approach this time. The sun had careened right over the roof of the school. Maybe he would get his answer up there. He quickly changed course and made his way to the "hidden" roof access stairway that everyone knew about. Even though he had only been at the school six hours, he had kept his eyes and ears open. Karl made absolutely sure that he was not being followed before entering the stairwell. Creeping up the darkened stairs, he was very cautious because if anything powerful enough to move the sun was waiting for him, he was going to take precautions. Karl just so happened to keep a small canister of pepper spray in a secluded pocket of his backpack (just in case of criminals, of course). He removed it before entering and now had one finger on the top, ready to blast whoever it was square in the face.

To his surprise, the door was opened a smidge proving his theory that someone or something was lurking on school property. When Karl finally got the courage to bust through the door and face the being, he saw something that he couldn't even comprehend—a very beautiful girl. The most random thing that could happen on a Monday afternoon was happening on a Monday afternoon. She had wavy, beach-blond hair that fell to her lower back. She wore a bright white flowing dress that reached a little past her knees. She appeared content but also cautious since an elementary school kid was pointing a spray bottle in the direction of her eyeballs. Even through all of that, she seemed pleased that he was there. From Karl's point of view, she didn't seem quite human. She looked at him. Her gaze seemed calm, happy even. Karl lowered his weapon and took a baby step forward. He opened his mouth and nearly let out a scared "hello" but startlingly enough, she beat him to it.

"Lovely afternoon," the girl said.

It was not the first thing that came to his mind when he thought of the day he was having and not something he would expect to hear from someone he barged in on, but yes, it was lovely afternoon indeed. Karl answered with a smile, "Yes, it's quite nice." He had no clue where "it's quite nice" came from, but he suspected that it was because she had a British accent. It only seemed right to act a little (a ton) more sophisticated than he normally would. The girl seemed not to hear the conversation Karl was having in his head, so he settled on following up with a polite introduction. "My name is Karl Weston. I'm attending school here. Sorry to bother you. I was just in an exploring mood today, if you know what I mean." Karl imagined smacking himself across the face, feeling the burn. To his utter relief, she laughed and nodded her head up and down, signaling that she did, in fact, understand. Her unexpected answer made the awkward young boy more comfortable about barging in, pepper spray a-blazing, to her secret retreat, which, incidentally, had an amazing view of the sky.

"My name is Rarity, and I do have that feeling occasionally, Karl Weston," she said as her beautiful accent floated on the breeze. She invited him to sit next to her on the edge of the stone-covered roof, their feet hanging over the side.

Karl didn't know it just yet, but he had just found a really amazing best friend that he would remember for the rest of his life. He never did find out what happened to the sun that day, but sometimes it's best to leave the world's mysteries unsolved. Every day after school, Karl visited Rarity at her hideout on the roof. He told his mom that he was participating in the school choir so she wouldn't worry. They did so many fun things together like telling stories and acting out impromptu (and pretty hilarious) skits. Rarity never talked about where she came from. Mostly, she listened to Karl and gave him her opinions, ideas, or kind words. Karl appreciated how much she let him speak his mind but longed to hear her background story.

As Zennith told his story, his friends assumed that Rarity was just a regular schoolgirl that he had an adorable crush on. Zen didn't say otherwise, but he knew that this experience was way more important than some crush. He wanted them to understand but knew they just couldn't. So he cleared his mind and continued with the story.

One day after school, Rarity wasn't there. Karl looked high and low, but she was nowhere to be found. Every day after school, Karl searched for his missing companion. He hoped that one day she would come back and explain everything. The weeks dragged on. Karl went to the roof less and less; until, finally, he stopped going altogether. Thankfully, the bus ride was always quiet. It was the only time he really had a chance to think.

Creeeeek! The old bus doors opened. It was May, and school was almost over for the summer. The sweet breeze lifted his ruffled hair and gave a sense of calmness to his troubled mind. Only two other kids got off with him, not necessarily good people to make conversations with unless you loved sports. As he walked, Karl looked down at his now worn-out black shoes, absentmindedly analyzing their structure and design. Then he began to feel a bright warming sensation as if the sun were glowing right behind him. Karl turned around to see his lovely friend standing on the gravel walkway in front of his house. He threw off his backpack, and they shared a warm hug. Karl couldn't remember the last time someone his own age hugged him that long.

After about three minutes of happy silence, Rarity began to explain her absence. Karl's mom, who was watching her son's happiness unfold right before her eyes, leaned out the door to wave hello and swiftly excused herself to "make lemonade" so they could talk. Even though there were hundreds of mixed emotions traveling through Karl's brain, he tried his very best to listen to every detail.

"I am so, so sorry I didn't give you any sort of warning of my absence," she began. "The thing is, I got captured."

Karl was stunned. "What happened to you, Rarity?"

"While you were at school one day I was taking a short walk through the school garden and literally stopped to smell some flowers. Then a bunch of scary people in suits grabbed my arm and took me to a strange place."

"Wow! Was it an orphanage?" Karl asked.

She nodded. "They put me in a small room with some other kids our age and just shut the door. About a week later, I was summoned downstairs to the office. A family was sitting in chairs in front of a desk. There was a father, mother, and their young daughter. I didn't know what was going on. There was something about adoption and a signature. Pretty soon, the father and office person were shaking hands."

"Wow! How did you escape that situation?" Karl was now very much intrigued about what this brave young girl had gone through and felt awful, forever thinking she had purposefully abandoned him.

"Despite my constant protesting, these people took me to their home. The whole time, I was thinking about how worried you'd be when I didn't show up the next afternoon. They were, thankfully, a nice family and took good care of me, but I still longed to be on my own like I was before. . . " She trailed off and let silence fill the air. There they sat, just looking beyond the trees in front of them. But then she startled him with a sudden change of tone. "I never knew where I came from. I just sort of knew that I could survive without anyone else. So I ran away in the middle of the night. It was pretty easy actually." Rarity exhaled, took a sip of the cool lemonade Karl's mom gave them, and set the glass down beside her. "It is so nice to see you again. I'm glad you know why I disappeared. But there is something I should tell you. I'm leaving again."

Karl almost spit out his remaining lemonade. "What? Why?"

"I have to, Karl. If they come searching for me, it will happen again and my life will be changed. I just don't want that. For your sake and mine, please let me go."

Karl was practically sobbing when she finished. After so many months of waiting and finally getting to see her again, she was leaving. This time for good. He couldn't speak. It finally dawned on him that she loved him enough to say good-bye. After some denial, he realized that he loved her too. Even at ten years old, he knew it was real. Rarity stood up, and Karl swiftly followed. They hugged again, even longer than before.

"I'll never forget you, Karl Weston." She slipped the ring she always wore into his hand then disappeared into the dense woods.

I'll never forget you either, Rarity, he thought. And he never did.

18

OUT OF THE BOAT AND
ONTO THE ISLAND

As Zennith finished his story, the clouds cleared so they threw off the towel and took a look around.

"I think we found our next stop," said Dagon, pointing.

The island looked dark and gloomy in the evening light. The friends agreed it would be safer to go early in the morning before monsters or scary beings were done with their "beauty rest" (Dagon thought of that one), not that it would help much. Someone would undoubtedly set off a trap or snap a branch, sending newly awakened beasts charging after them. They knew that they were on a time-sensitive schedule and waiting would set them back a few hours, but morning it was.

A small beam of sunlight burst through the window and warmed Zen's face. He woke up and remembered what they all agreed to do this morning. "Time to attack this piece of land and conquer some monsters," he mumbled. A few minutes later he was up and around, putting clothes on and thinking of ways to wake his friends. He knew that everyone else on the ship was sleeping contently. He didn't even have to check. *I'm sure they will love me for this*, he thought as he opened the door to Dagon's bedroom.

Zennith figured that his longest friend would stay angry with him the least amount of time so he started there. "Knock, knock!" He hit the door before opening it to reveal Dagon's sleeping form. Dagon was not the most attractive sleeper. Half the covers were on the floor, and his mouth was wide open. "This is going to be interesting," Zennith sighed. He scanned the room, and eventually, his eyes landed on a light switch. This sparked an idea. "Sorry, man," he said in advance. His mom used to use that technique on him all the time, and it generally demonstrated a high-working percentage. Zennith flipped it on and walked out just as he heard a groan coming from the bed.

Next were Maylis's quarters. This was going to be a bit harder because of two things. One, Maylis was still on edge about the whole *ring* situation. Two, Zennith already witnessed Aidryan and Dagon wake Maylis up. It always ended with one of them being flung across the room and hitting an expensive vase or something. As Zennith made his way over to Maylis's king-size bed, he noticed that his room was a bit bigger than the other travelers' bunks. That was certainly going to be a conversation for another time.

To wake Maylis, Zennith chose to go with the lights-on method again because he would be far away from his potentially angry friend. Before blasting Maylis with light, Zennith decided to take advantage of the fact that Maylis was passed out under a cheetah-skin comforter, wearing a matching silk pajama outfit. Apparently, they came with the deluxe room. Zennith stepped over to the drawer where Maylis kept his phone and quietly opened it. He snapped almost twenty pictures before reviewing his work and placing the phone back in the drawer. Even though Zennith had gotten defensive about the ring and the interruptions, he and Maylis were still friends with an unbreakable bond. In some weird way, Zennith considered the sneaky pictures a peace offering.

Since Maylis was still asleep Zen figured it wouldn't hurt to look around. He felt a bit uncomfortable while he was going through his friend's stuff, but Zen sort of felt he had earned the right to snoop as of yesterday's constant interruptions. The only thing Zennith really knew about his Laminian heritage was that he, Dagon, and Aidryan needed to leave when they were all about a year old because an evil wizard threatened Dagon's father, the king. Maybe Maylis's room had some more answers. After searching every nook and cranny, Zennith didn't find anything interesting except a pair of socks labeled "Made in Lamin." Zen turned on the lights on his way out the door. He didn't want to stick around to witness Maylis's venom.

Next on the wake-up call list was Aidryan. As soon as Zen stepped foot in his friend's room, he decided that this was going to be the scariest to invade. First of all, he felt awkward going into a girl's room even though he knew her fairly well. Second, she had better reflexes than both of the other boys and maybe even Maylis combined. For all her parading around in dresses and sporting perfectly combed hair at all times, she could become a vicious warrior princess in one second flat. But despite the danger of waking the beast, he had a job to do. One of the first things Zen noticed when he entered was the way she was sleeping. There she was with her head gently resting on the pillow and her legs stretched out below her. Her room was the cleanest place he had ever seen. Books were stacked neatly in alphabetical order, and a laptop sat on her organized desk alongside pencils separated by color. But the floor was the scariest of all. It was so clean, he could have licked it. Zennith finally pried his eyes off the neatness and remembered the reason why he was here in the first place. He tiptoed back into the hallway and pulled the door behind him just enough to allow his hand to fit through. He flicked on the lights.

"Hey! Who did that?" Zen yelled. Then he ran for his life. Zennith could hear her screaming all the way down the hall.

Like a cockroach, Ryan waited in the hold. The phone call he had with Ty went well. Now Ty was recruiting an army of teens that would gladly smack the magic right out of those pesky kids. Meanwhile, Ryan was enjoying being secluded from all natural light and human interaction. There was even some food in the bags that surrounded him and water bottles as well. He hunkered down, waiting for Ty and his teen army to arrive.

The four explorers hid their boat in a secure place behind some trees in a lagoon and wandered into the dense woods in search of a clue. The map indicated this was a stop on their journey, and a Laminian treasure would be here for them to collect. They all hoped it would be a "get in, get out" situation. Although the island looked imposing, if you took away the looming clouds and dead quiet, it was actually rather pretty. Zennith admired the powdery sand beaches and swaying palm trees.

As soon as they stepped foot on the island, Dagon had taken it upon himself to be in control. No one really minded because he was good at it.

"This is a good spot to rest," Dagon decided.

"I agree," said Aidryan.

"It doesn't seem too buggy," Maylis chimed in.

"It sure has some nice scenery. I mean, look at this place! Guys?" Zennith looked around, finding Dagon and the rest of his friends crouching behind a big boulder.

"Yes, I believe this is a great island for sightseeing," said a low voice.

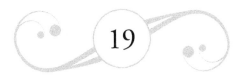

19

FRIEND OR FOE?

Standing behind Zennith was a man dressed in a magician's costume.

"Welcome to the Isle of Gobique!" he announced. "Why do you look so scared? Haven't you ever seen a magician before?"

Mr. Gobique, the island man, looked hurt, then indicated for the jittery kids to follow him. They looked at each other and figured that no one wanted to be turned into anything unnatural—now or *ever*—so they decided it was best to just go along. Plus, befriending this island man and making him an ally could prove helpful in the future.

Dagon was expecting the islander to live in a little beat-up shack near some overgrown trees. He also anticipated that the self-described magician practiced pulling rabbits out of knockoff hats and sawed animals (or unlucky humans) in half. But what he saw made his jaw drop to the ground. The others were having the same moment.

"Oh yeah, this thing. Well, it's really nothing much. You should see my place in Peru," the island magician boasted.

At this point the companions didn't care if he were trying to capture them. (They already prepared for that.) Maylis, Aidryan, Zennith, and Dagon just wanted to explore the magician's sprawling mansion as soon as possible. The inside was just as breathtaking as the outside. The strange man explained that he created and sold magic rings that teleported people to different realms and made a magnificent fortune from it.

"So, sir—" Aidryan began.

"Sam Gobique," he declared.

"Oh, okay, Mr. Gobique. Do you know this island pretty well?"

"I know that the island is five miles long and has three hundred unique types of fruit trees," he replied. "It is home to a variety of lizards and snakes, some undiscovered by scientists. The temperature peaks at a balmy ninety degrees, and the best spot for suntanning is about two miles from here by a grove of palm trees nestled beside a crystal clear freshwater stream."

"Excuse us a moment please, Mr. Gobique," Aidryan said and turned to her friends for a private huddle. "Okay, so this guy might be helpful. Dagon's dad sent us here for a reason, so we might as well try asking Mr. G for help."

Maylis nodded. "Yes, but it could get tricky. Islands around these parts are known for being . . . mysterious."

"We still don't know if we can even trust him. For all we know, he could be a sick freak who has a very good taste in island mansions," Dagon added.

"I am aware of that, Dag, but this is the best chance we've had since we got here," Aidryan concluded.

They broke out of their group huddle and turned to face Mr. Gobique. Aidryan wondered how long they had been discussing the situation when she laid her eyes on four plates stacked high with delicious-looking food sitting on a table in front of them. Stomach grumblings came from everyone. It was at that moment they realized how desperate they were for a proper meal.

"Maybe it isn't such a bad idea to get help from this guy after all," Zennith exclaimed.

The others nodded their heads in agreement and began munching hungrily on their gourmet meals while Mr. G sat back and watched his hospitality speak for itself. After a glorious meal, Mr. Gobique showed them more of the huge mansion.

Maylis was the most curious about this place because he had never heard of this man before. Why would King Klayric send them here? He suspected it was some sort of test.

"I wonder if those angry teens we dominated with water balloons will ever come back to settle the score," Maylis mused aloud.

His friends were apparently not in the mood to rehash that experience, so Maylis only got half answers from each of them. He still wasn't entirely sure what they were supposed to be searching for in this mansion but soon got lost in his thoughts as the tour continued up to the second floor.

"As you climb this winding staircase, which is covered with an imported Persian rug, you can marvel at my custom window that looks out to the opposite side of the island! This is my favorite spot to think, unwind, and relax with some tea," said Mr. Gobique. He stood silent, appreciating the view for a moment, then led his guests down a long hallway of mirrors. He stopped again and turned around to face them. "It seems you have arrived at my island at a rather inopportune time. I do not want to startle you or anything dreadful like that. However, I believe there is a storm coming." He said *storm* in a particularly dramatic voice. "I wouldn't normally bother you with this information, but a *storm* like this only comes once or twice a year, and I am very glad of that. You are welcome to stay here tonight. I assure you that this house is as sturdy as I am." That last statement wasn't reassuring, but it was definitely a gracious offer.

Back to the huddle.

"What do you think, you guys? It's a pretty sweet deal, and it would be tough getting back to the boat now anyway because of the storm," Dagon reasoned.

"Yeah, I'm in!" Zen said. "It will let us regroup and stuff. Plus, it would be nice to not sleep in a swaying boat for once."

"That's true," agreed Aidryan. "Maylis, what do you suggest we do?"

Maylis sighed and looked over at the excited girl. "I still don't completely trust this guy. I think I will sleep on the boat and make a shield spell just in case the storm wrecks my chances of a good night's sleep. You three can stay here and pamper yourselves, but contact me immediately if you feel threatened."

Dagon and his friends watched him go. When they turned around, their host was nowhere to be seen. They frantically asked each other the last time anyone saw him. Luckily, moments later, Mr. Gobique poked his head out from a doorway and called for them to come check out their new digs.

The first word that was spoken from each of the companion's mouth was a flabbergasted, "*Wow!*" The room itself was huge. It was painted a pleasant cream color, and windows taller than Dagon lined three walls. A plush light-blue rug spread out before them like a red carpet. There were four full-size beds with curtains. Talk about taking privacy to the next level. Aidryan rushed over to the bed with the rosy pink comforter. She was obviously claiming this bed, and neither Dagon nor Zennith could argue.

"I hope you enjoy your accommodations. I thought this room would be a perfect fit for everyone. Oh, and by the way, there is a snack bar in the connecting room, which you are welcome to eat from at any time. I'll let you get settled in. But wait, where is the other boy who was with you earlier? I was certain I picked a room with the right amount of beds."

"Oh, he is going to stay on the boat for tonight. He wants to make sure that it doesn't get destroyed in the storm," Dagon informed him.

"Are you absolutely positive that he will be all right in this terrible storm?" Mr. Gobique asked, crinkling his forehead.

"Oh, yeah, sir. Maylis can handle anything," Aidryan responded with confidence.

"Okay, well, have a wonderful evening. I will show you around more tomorrow," he offered.

"Great, thanks!" Zen replied quickly.

The island man smiled and closed the door securely behind him.

"It's only seven o'clock. We can still do stuff before we go to sleep," Dagon suggested.

His friends all agreed. Aidryan started checking out the closets full of clothes, while Zennith destroyed the snack bar. Dagon looked at his compass and murmured, "I'm almost home, Dad." As Zennith and Aidryan made themselves at home, Dagon announced that he was going to take a shower and change out of his old clothes.

"Okay, bro, no problem. NO WAY! There are cheese puffs over here!" Zennith made a beeline for the cheesy snacks. Dagon and Aidryan laughed. Zennith always had a knack for making everyone feel happy.

The travelers ate and tried on as many ridiculous combinations of clothes as they possibly could. Then they climbed into bed and began to wind down as more and more yawns dotted their conversation. Soon, Dagon and Aidryan heard Zennith snoring loudly in his red-and-blue Spiderman sheets. He was surrounded by various delicacies from around the world, but he reserved a special place for the cheese puffs container so he could wrap his arm around it. It took nearly fifteen minutes for Aidryan and Dagon to reposition him in such a way that his snoring wasn't so thunderous. Afterward, they collapsed on the floor in front of his bed and leaned their tired backs against the footboard, catching their breath.

"I can't believe we have magical powers and still struggled to make our friend stop snoring," Dagon said. "Being magical in general still feels kind of—"

"Strange," Aidryan finished. "I've never imagined anything close to what's happened in the past month. We never could have stood up to Ty and Makayla like that before. We were awesome!"

They both paused, soaking it all in.

"I want to meet my dad," Dagon sighed.

"Yeah, I want to meet my uncle too. I'll probably ask him so many questions his crown will fly right off of his head," Aidryan joked playfully.

Dagon laughed.

Aidryan shrugged. "I wonder how your mother felt when she left to come back to the States."

"Yeah . . " Dagon trailed off.

"Hey, Dagon?"

"Yes?"

"We have a big day of exploring tomorrow, I'd hate to be sleepwalking through it."

"Okay, you're probably right."

Both cousins stumbled to their feet and made their way to their comfortable beds before crashing onto their pillows and closing their eyes.

"Good night, Dagon."

"'Night, Aidryan."

20

A Very Destructive Storm

Ryan had no idea a storm was coming. Below deck, where he was hiding, was surprisingly comfortable. After living there for a while, the saltwater smell and stuffy air had grown on him. There were also plenty of things to keep him occupied while he waited for his friends to show up and confront those weird magic kids. Ryan had never been much of a fighter, but he was loyal to his friends, which is why he agreed to become a spy. Besides, he would be a hero when he told Ty all the secret information that Dagon and his cousin had been keeping. He was a big reason why Ty and Makayla would succeed.

As he made his way to the yacht, Maylis second-guessed his decision to leave his friends. He trudged through the dense jungle of trees and exotic flowers that looked more or less like they were going to grow eyes and eat him whole. Yes, the kids had learned how to use and control magic successfully in a controlled environment, but there were so many more nuances that hadn't even come into play yet. Maylis had no idea how they would handle things under circumstances like this. He considered the museum escapade to be a level one. What would happen to them in a level ten situation?

His mind then moved on to the whereabouts of Erex, the sorcerer who was still at large. Banishment obviously didn't hold him long. What made Erex so unpredictably evil was that he could disappear for as long as it took to guarantee that when he struck, it would be a surprise. Personally, Maylis had never seen Erex in all his terrible glory, but Dagon's father sure had.

"Ah, Dagon, full of spirit and courage. He is going to make a great king one day," Maylis said out loud. "But I can't believe he's friends with someone as silly and irritating as Zen." Maylis laughed at the joke. Zennith was a good, loyal companion to Dagon and would make a superb second in command. He and Aidryan would certainly be of great use to Dagon when it came time for him to step up and take the crown. Maylis had no doubt about it.

Maylis liked to think when he was alone. It helped him unwind and feel more in control. As he thought about all these things, he became less aware of his surroundings. So when a giant oak tree stood in the path of the distracted young boy, he was a goner. *Thump!* The collision caused a few branches to break, and a startled squirrel vacated the tree using Maylis's head as a trampoline.

Back at the mansion, Aidryan's voice broke the silence.

"I wonder if Maylis is okay. And what about Rarity? Will she be safe outside in this storm?"

"She is, after all, deck furniture so she's used to being in the elements," Dagon reminded her. "I'm sure they'll both be just fine, but I'm hungry. Midnight snack?"

"Sure, sounds good."

Zennith was still out cold, despite the fact that the superhero bedsheet was not covering him anymore. Aidryan and Dagon took that as a hint that they didn't have to worry about crunching too loudly.

Maylis had recovered from his embarrassing tree hug and was just a little way from being safely on the boat. The trip back had been a lot longer than he expected. He looked up at the darkening sky and began to run. The island man may not be trustworthy, but he was right about one thing—a storm was definitely brewing. Maylis usually wasn't afraid of storms, but everything on this journey was far from ordinary. He expected the impact of this whirlwind to be no different. He stopped by an old tree to catch his breath before his last big sprint.

"I really need to hit the gym when I get back," he wheezed.

The storm was practically on top of him when he reached the boat. He looked back to see the clouds circling in behind him, about to strike. He kicked himself for giving up the chance to sleep in an actual bed with the comfort of his friends by his side. He put his hand on the door to go below deck and turned the knob. It was locked. Maylis remembered asking Dagon to put a locking spell on the boat when they left. After all, they didn't know what to expect from an island that wasn't on a regular map. Maylis searched his brain for more options. While he tried to come up with a possible solution, the rain, thunder, and roaring wind decided they'd been waiting too long and set themselves free. Maylis panicked and decided to head back to Mr. Gobique's mansion. Since he had been through these woods twice before, it wouldn't take as long to get there—he hoped. After a muddy trek and a run-in with a ten-legged spider, he finally spotted lights in the distance.

"*Aha!*" Maylis smiled through the hair that was plastered all over his face. To his grave disappointment, the front door was locked. He turned to the next best option. There was a vine growing up the side of the house that happened to be extremely close to the window where he thought his friends might be. Maylis didn't waste any time. He took a running leap, landed on the sturdy vine, and began to climb. He was working his way up the vine fairly smoothly until he heard voices. Frozen with fear, he peeked into a rain-pelted window and could just make out the magician walking up the staircase. At first, this confused Maylis. Why would Mr. Gobique be talking to himself like that? His question was soon answered when the man bent down to pick up a small Labrador puppy. Maylis thought two things. One, *that is a cute dog!* And two, *dogs can sniff out people with no problem.*

Maylis tried his best to blend into the green vine (challenging in a yellow outfit), stay still, and listen. He balanced himself on the vine just out of view of the window and leaned in to hear their conversation over the pouring rain. Maylis was surprised he could get away with performing even one of these skills without falling. The magician reached the top of the carpeted stairs and (of course) glanced out the same window where Maylis was hanging. Maylis pressed himself against the trusty green vine, not even daring to breathe. He wished he were the dog so he could be warm and dry and have innocent eyes so that he could get away with anything. He thought of using magic but his concentration was a bit shattered, so he just decided to lay low and act like a secret agent for this one.

"Are you kidding me?" Ryan yelled and hung up the phone in a huff. Ty had just informed him that they were going to reach him later than expected because of the crazy storm that was tossing their boat like a Frisbee across the water. Subsequent to their frustrating conversation, Ryan started to get freaked out. All the protection he had with him was a Laminian book of magical spells and a flashlight from a phone that hadn't been charged in days.

"Okay, I'll . . . I'll be fine. It's just a storm. How bad could it actually be?" The short pep talk helped him relax a little. Unfortunately for Ryan, however, the pep talk didn't prepare him for the giant flash of light and thunderous crash that jostled the boat. Ryan screamed.

Uh, what was that? Maylis thought after hearing a sudden shriek in the night. The shriek was followed by a loud snapping sound, a sound he had been dreading the entire duration of his climb. "Oh, lords of Lamin," he uttered. The bottom part of the vine had broken free from the house and was now swaying back and forth in the gale.

The island man opened the window slightly. The wind tugged Maylis to the right as Mr. Gobique looked to the left. Next, the wind pulled him left when Mr. Gobique craned his neck to the right. Maylis clung to the shutter and managed to stay out of view. Mr. Gobique shrugged, closed the window, and walked down the hall, still talking to his pooch.

21

PURPLE EVERYWHERE

The next crack of lightning woke Aidryan up. She sat on the edge of her bed, debating whether she should even try to go back to sleep. She never liked storms or anything she had absolutely no control over. She glanced over at the other beds. The room was almost completely dark except for a small blue night-light that Dagon used. She could see that Zennith was about as scared as a stone wall. Dagon was still. She couldn't tell whether his eyes were open or not. Somewhere, a clock chimed two. Aidryan wondered how anyone besides Zennith could sleep through the noise, so she did what any other normal person would do if they found themselves in a mysterious place.

She slipped a fluffy robe over her pajamas and tiptoed across the floor to the door. The halls were long and black. Before she bumped into anyone or anything, she conjured a spell that lit the tip of her finger, illuminating her steps. She didn't know exactly what she expected to find on her adventure, but she was prepared for anything. Luckily, Mr. Gobique was organized. Above many of the doors, Aidryan saw labels engraved on wooden plaques. She figured that if she lived alone in this giant house on a secret island away from civilization, she would also want to keep track of what was in all these rooms.

Aidryan's fingerlight was more useful than she anticipated. It had already kept her from knocking a stone head off a pedestal and down a staircase that led to the kitchen. It didn't, however, prevent her from backing up into a purple wall. When she looked closer, she became aware of the fact that it was a shade of purple she'd never seen before—if it even were purple. For a few minutes, she stared in awe at this wondrous wall. She just couldn't tear her eyes away from its mesmerizing color. Aidryan placed her hand on the wall lightly as if it were going to move at her touch. She slid her hand along and followed it to two black doors with crystal handles, which added to the whole creepiness factor. She blew out her finger and touched one of the handles with a smirk. The one thing she was absolutely certain about was that she was going to find out what was behind it.

The one thing in the entire universe that Aidryan was not expecting to find behind that door of destiny was an empty room, but that was what she got. Nothing. Just an empty lit chamber painted the same color as the one outside it. The room was rectangular and about the same size as a small living room. The ceiling barely reached a foot above Aidryan's head. Although disappointed about not finding any treasure, Aidryan was extremely relieved that nothing tried to kill her. She knew that the mansion was home to someone who called himself a magician, so she figured he would never just have an empty room like that. There had to be a secret passage somewhere. She padded across the smooth wooden floor, stood close to one of the murals on the far wall, and commenced her analyzing.

Plastered over the top of the strange purple color were gold-and-black designs that looked like little eyeballs looking out at her. Aidryan walked slowly down the wall, pressing her cold fingers against the paint. The texture massaged her fingers as they glided over the intricate patterns. Suddenly, her thumb rubbed something that felt different. It had caught on to a tiny flaw in the repeating pattern. Aidryan lifted her thumb and leaned in closer to the wall.

There was an eye that stood out from the rest. Every other eyeball appeared to be looking straight at her, but this one was clearly looking to the left. She had found her clue, a big fat clue that couldn't even look her in the eye. Just for kicks, she pressed her shaky finger up against the distinctive eyeball. *Snap!* After recovering from a slight heart attack, she saw that the eyeball had switched directions and was now staring up at the ceiling. She followed its gaze. Smiling, she said, "I love magic."

On the low ceiling was written one word, and for once the directions were crystal clear— "Jump." Aidryan had a pretty good idea of what was about to happen, which made the whole situation much scarier.

"Well, here goes nothing," she muttered through clenched teeth. "Three . . . two . . . one . . . Go!" Aidryan jumped.

As soon as Aidryan was airborne, time went in slow motion. She could see her surroundings closing in on her as the room got smaller and more compact. Being relieved was an understatement when her feet finally touched the familiar wooden floor again. But this time when she looked around, instead of the mysterious purple color surrounding her, she was in a tiny dark room with the only light source coming from a hole above. When Aidryan's eyes adjusted, she could see trinkets of every different shape, size, and color. At first, everything seemed to meld together so that it was hard to make out the designs decorating some of the golden goblets and vintage-looking silverware. When Aidryan took a closer look at one of the glasses, she noticed a Laminian symbol that was partially rubbed off. *Does Mr. Gobique know about Lamin? Does he know that we are from Lamin?*

To calm herself down, she decided to scan the rest of the items for more clues. Maybe she could find the treasure they were sent here for in the first place. Her thoughts were interrupted by a small beam of light peeking behind one of the bookcases that lined the walls. She cautiously walked over to it, slightly tilting her head so the beam didn't interrupt her line of vision. The item that was causing the bright illumination was actually one of the smallest treasures in the room. Aidryan felt a strange connection to it. The coin was about the size of four quarters combined and had a Laminian symbol pressed into it, just like one of the pictures in the history book Maylis gave her. She dusted it off and lightly pressed her teeth on one side. She had taken a class about identifying metals and just from one small bite, she knew exactly what it was. Aidryan flashed back to her first day of the metal detectors class she took when she was about eight years old.

Aidryan sat front and center waiting for instructions. Her teacher was seated at his desk staring out into the classroom full of nerdy kids. He waited until everyone was silent before he stood and began class.

"My name is Mr. Woodbranch," he said sternly. Mr. Woodbranch was quite a tall man so the kids' necks would hurt at the end of his classes. It was a bit easier if he was sitting down, but he rarely felt the need to sit down while teaching. His eyes were dark blue, and his hair was sandy brown. Today he was wearing khakis and a short-sleeved, navy-blue button-down shirt. Everyone knew him as the quiet antisocial teacher who gave more homework than all the other teachers combined. Mr. Woodbranch cleared his throat. "Today is going to be a simple lesson about identifying the substance in front of you."

Aidryan never forgot the next thing he said. "I want you to taste it. Press the edge of it with your teeth and tell me what you think. Don't bite too hard, of course. Just enough to get a flavor."

Young Aidryan was uncertain why she had to do this and wondered if it were poison and if this tall teacher were out to kill his students, but her curiosity got the best of her so she just shrugged and lightly bit down.

"The taste you are now familiar with is platinum. It is an extremely dense chemical element discovered by Antonio de Ulloa in 1735."

"Cool," Aidryan whispered.

Aidryan had enough adventuring for one night and didn't want Dagon to worry that someone had taken her. She slipped the coin into her robe pocket and rummaged through the other objects one more time for a souvenir. There was a cloak resting on a dramatic wing chair. It was the same mysterious purple color that was on the walls. "This will do," she said as she wrapped it around herself. Just then, she heard footsteps coming down the hall. *Oh, I wish I were back in my room!* she thought. A moment later, Aidryan was back in her room.

Maylis stood on the windowsill, soaking wet. Dagon was helping him down. Both of them looked at her and froze with their mouths open in shock. Zennith's mouth may have been open in shock, but it was hard to tell because it was stuffed with candy. No doubt the most shocking thing to Aidryan was the fact that Zennith was actually awake.

"Hey!" she said.

22

CONFESSIONS

"So what did I miss?" Aidryan said sarcastically.

"Pretty much everything," Dagon answered.

"I bet we all have many, many questions for one another," Maylis put in as he eyeballed Aidryan's fancy cloak.

"*Yeghughhuhh*," Zennith added as pieces of food dribbled from his overstuffed mouth. When he realized this was, in fact, not the most attractive look, he spit half the wet candy into a nearby trash can. "Who would like to kick things off?"

They all laughed and helped Maylis dry off.

"So, Maylis, what terrible creature chased you back to comfort and luxury?" Zen asked.

Maylis shifted in his seat and ignored all the giggles from his friends. "Yeah, well, you see . . . I kind of became buddies with a very large tree." He got confused looks from everyone but had no intention of continuing with that story so he explained about the boat's locked door. "I was somewhat close to the boat when the storm started closing in on me and was able to reach it without much trouble. But I forgot that it was on magical lockdown, so I wasn't able to get in. I had nowhere else to go so I came back here."

"So when did you bond with the tree?" Aidryan asked.

"Oh, that was on the way back there. I wasn't looking where I was going and ran right into it."

It was as if a huge container of laughing gas had been thrown into the room. Maylis realized what he just admitted, and his face reddened prominently. After his friends settled down (it took a while), he described his vine-climbing adventure. He laughed at the part when he became a ninja, dodging the magician and seeing him talking to his dog. Everyone let out another happy chuckle.

Then it was Aidryan's turn. "I think I found what we're looking for," she said. "I think it originated from Lamin because of the carvings around it and the way it shines. It even tastes like platinum!" She whipped aside the purple cloak, took the coin out of her robe pocket, and passed it around. She explained how the storm kept her up, how she found the secret room, and how she discovered the space full of treasures and trinkets by jumping.

Maylis was the last to examine the treasure. "Looks like we are one step closer to fulfilling our quest." He smiled. "It also appears that there is a single letter written on the back." He lifted the coin up to a lamp while the others gasped to see a Laminian letter *L*.

"Does this mean that the other treasures will have letters, and we have to spell out a word?" Dagon wondered.

"It seems so. I'm guessing the word is *Lamin*," Aidryan remarked.

Now it was Zen's turn for story time, but he didn't seem excited to share. "So I know this might be anticlimactic, after finding a clue and all, but here goes," he said solemnly as his friends inched closer to his chair. Zennith sighed and continued, "I also snuck out of the room to see Mr. Gobique." The kids gasped, especially Aidryan and Dagon who had seen how fast asleep he was. "I've always loved the magician's trade, so I thought maybe he could show me a few things."

When Zennith decided to take off in the middle of the night after noticing that Aidryan was gone, he wasn't positive it was a great idea. Zen wanted to talk with Mr. Gobique, but he had absolutely no idea where the magician was. He shivered just thinking about going down dark passages with only a magic wand and minimal alertness. With this in mind, Zennith decided to first search the rooms and hallways they had already seen. Zennith figured the kitchen was a good place to start because there were plenty of knives he could use if someone or something threatened him.

"The kitchen it is," he said aloud.

On his way to the kitchen, he hoped that the magician might actually come to him. Maybe magicians who live on islands have something that lets them know when someone wants to talk to them. That sounded like a good idea to Zennith so he promptly pulled an expensive-looking chair into the kitchen, sat down, and waited. After ten whole minutes, Zennith became impatient and turned around in his chair.

"WHOA!" Zennith yelled. "How did you know I was here?"

The island man was holding a flashlight and pointing it right at the boy. "I heard you bump into quite a bit of furniture on your way down here, Zennith."

"Oh."

Mr. Gobique patted his shoulder. "Oh, don't worry, it's okay. I'm glad I heard you."

Zennith imagined himself and Mr. Gobique dressed as shady characters meeting in a dark alley at midnight. This just proved that he had watched too many movies.

"So why are you sitting in my kitchen on this stormy night?" Mr. Gobique inquired.

Zen shifted in his chair. "I wanted to talk to you about—this is going to sound stupid."

"I will be the judge of that."

"Well, my dream ever since I could remember was to be an amazing magician."

"But you already are one."

"Yes, but—wait, how did you know I use magic?"

Mr. Gobique smiled. "Real magicians can sense the magic in other magicians. I'm going to go out on a limb here and say that you want to help your friends, but you feel like you could get in the way or not be useful, so you want to stay here so I can teach you more magic."

"Spot on."

"Thank you, thank you. I do try."

The island man sighed, "You remind me a great deal of me, Zennith. For that, I will train you. I can teach you complex spells, potions, and much more."

Zennith's face lit up as if a hundred lightning bugs had flown into his mouth, making his eyes glow. He was excited to learn from an expert that specialized in his dream. After all, Maylis was a Laminian native and a good teacher, Dagon was a caring leader and a prince, and Aidryan was smart and resourceful. It seemed to Zennith that he had no real contribution to add to the party.

Six eyes were on Zen as he finished his story (leaving out the part of him feeling useless) and didn't appear to want to leave his face.

"I'm sorry, guys, but I feel like this is the right path for me. I want to perform magic for a living, and I can learn how to do it here. Then I want to find Rarity—the girl, not the horse—and bring her back with me. This whole adventure was loads of fun but . . " He trailed off.

As much as everyone hated to admit it, Zennith was right. Dagon, for sure, knew about his dream to become a magician. It would be selfish and cruel to prevent him from fulfilling it. Aidryan was the first to break the silence. "Zen, we fully support your dreams and ambitions and . . . and I agree with you staying here to learn as much as you can about magic."

Zen let out a huge smile and hugged her tight. "You're the best, thank you!"

"Yeah, me too, buddy. I think you'll be a successful magician one day," Dagon added.

"Thanks, Dag. I know it will be weird having one less member aboard the *SS Maylinator* (small giggles from the kids and one confused Maylis), but I believe that you can collect the remaining clues and get to Lamin safely without me."

After a few more tight hugs and tears, they got into their comfortable beds and tried to squeeze in a few more hours of sleep before they left in the morning. Their plan was pretty straightforward, but it wouldn't be as fun without Zennith.

23

THE WINGED-HORSE ESCAPE

They were awakened by muffled shouts and banging coming from downstairs. Dagon attempted to get dressed, but after three hours of sleep, getting into his pants was harder than he imagined. The noises were getting louder and more impatient. They woke up Mr. Gobique as well. He was standing in the doorway wearing Ebenezer Scrooge pajamas with a wand quivering in his hand. As soon as the kids were dressed, they grabbed their wands and all five magicians crept down the long, regal staircase. They heard pounding on the grand front door.

"Why won't this thing open?" a girl said from outside.

"Because it's laced with magic, obviously," a boy explained.

"No, it's because it's locked, idiots," another spoke, clearly done with the conversation.

That made Dagon and Aidryan stop dead, almost causing Zennith, Maylis, and the island man to trip up the stairs. Now they knew who was behind those doors, which meant that Maylis was going to have to make a few more giant water balloons to win this fight.

"We are going to need a lot more than wands," Aidryan said as she glanced fearfully at Dagon.

"Okay, here's the plan. Aidryan, you, Mr. G, and I will attempt to hold them off. Zen, you and Maylis go upstairs and plot an escape. Make sure you pack all our stuff, especially the *special* things." Dagon gave them an unmistakable look.

The two boys nodded before dashing upstairs to carry out the prince's order.

You are the son of a magical king, Dagon thought. *Prove your worth.* He motioned to Aidryan to step back as he unlocked the heavy door. The opposing force that kept Dagon and his friends from a proper night's rest tumbled onto the floor in front of them. For a brief moment, nobody moved. It was like the calm before the devastating storm that was about to take place in the magician's mansion. Dagon stepped forward.

"Hello, Ty. I can't help but wonder why you are trespassing on an old man's property (a muffled gasp came from Mr. Gobique). Is it because you miss us or is it just because you need to prove how tough you are?"

Ty lunged forward. "Why you little—"

And the battle for justice began. Within the first few seconds, Mr. Gobique suffered a small-scale injury after being tackled to the ground by an angry teen. Aidryan had, of course, gone straight for Makayla, who was flanked by three of her comrades, all ready for action. Makayla took this opportunity to taunt her. "*Oooh!* You have a magic stick, how cute! I can totally use that to—*AAH!*"

Aidryan used a favorite spell that sent Makayla flying across the room. She loved her wand more and more every minute. She turned back to deal with Makayla's posse, but they were nowhere to be seen.

Dagon, on the other hand, was having a difficult time. One of his eyes was three shades of purple, his lip was bleeding, and he had a painful looking limp. Aidryan saw him struggling and rushed to his side. Three boys, including Ty, were still attacking Dagon and looked far from done.

Ty laughed. "Thanks for joining us, Aidryan. I was just telling your cousin over here how my good friend Ryan stowed away
on your ship and led us right to you. He also found quite an interesting book of yours."

Ryan threw the book hard at Dagon, making him stag-
ger backwards and fall ungracefully on the hard floor. His fists
clenched, his body shook, and his busted lip quivered with resolve.
Dagon handed the book and his wand to Aidryan and stood up. "I
don't ever want to see you again! Get out, get out!" Dagon yelled,
causing the lights to flicker and the insulation to rumble.

Aidryan stood beside him and faced Ty. Mr. Gobique had
recovered and was taking his frustration out on the unfortunate
adolescent who tackled him. The island man sent the boy flying
over their heads and right into Ty.

Zennith and Maylis got a good head start on activating the
plan. Zennith gathered all their belongings in one messy pile while
Maylis ran to the window to confirm that his friendly helper, the
vine, was ready to assist. Zennith ran down the hall and peeked
downstairs just in time to see Mr. G send the unfortunate teen
flying across the room. *I can't wait to learn that spell,* he thought.
He ran back to their room and received quite a shock. Sticking her
white head through the window was Rarity, the pegasus Aidryan
created from the deck chair. Zen's timing was impeccable because
the way Maylis and the horse were positioned looked like they were
posing for a portrait commissioned to hang in Dagon's palace.

Zennith coughed. "So I'm guessing you found a way off the
island?"

Maylis nodded. "It's time to help our friends!"

"Let's do this!" Zen shouted as the two boys busted out of the
room, wands blazing.

The horse must have thought they were crazy. About thirty
seconds after their dramatic exit, Zen and Maylis were back in
their room, looking slightly embarrassed. Aidryan and Dagon,
who were crossing their arms and smirking, followed them.

"So I guess you can take care of yourselves," Zennith grumbled.

Dagon and Aidryan stopped in their tracks when they caught sight of their ride. Strapped to Rarity's back was a beautiful carriage fit for royalty. This horse had come prepared. Realization hit when they remembered that one special person was not going to be joining them. Everyone went around, giving out hugs and kind words. When the three friends were finished putting their belongings inside the carriage, something happened that delayed their takeoff. Who should come crawling back up the stairs but the head of the water balloon throwing committee, Ty.

"I am not letting you get away from me a *second* time," he scoffed. Evidently, he wasn't entirely recovered from his fight with Dagon and Aidryan because he didn't seem to notice the giant winged horse in the window staring at him. Using the last of his might, Ty charged for Dagon and his friends.

Zennith shoved Ty out of the way and shouted, "Go! Go! Go!"

Dagon, Aidryan, and Maylis jumped into the carriage; and the powerful beast took off.

24

RARITY

The carriage was round and decorated with gold-and-purple trim, and the inside was a beautiful pale lavender. The harness that attached Rarity to the circular coach was made of regal gold-and-purple leather. The view from this height was incredible too. Vibrant sunlight lit up the windows, and they heard waves crashing on the bright blue ocean many feet below them. They saw puffy clouds and an array of pinks, oranges, and intense reds surrounding the ascending sun.

Aidryan fiddled with the coin, tracing the Laminian *L* over and over. The gentle glide through the clouds was much more relaxing than being rudely bombarded by a bunch of ruthless teenage maniacs. At least she didn't have to worry about them anymore because Mr. Gobique and Zennith had everything under control. She was just afraid of a few tiny things. One, would Zennith's new mentor actually benefit him and not lock him up so no one could ever find him? (Aidryan's mind liked to imagine the worst scenarios). Two, the reason they actually found the way to Sarina and her talking book was mostly because of Zen. What if they needed someone with his type of silly brain to figure out a puzzle? Aidryan decided not to dwell on it because it was making her a nervous wreck. Although he was Dagon's friend first, she had grown to really like Zennith. The last thing she wanted was for him to get hurt in any way. At least she had two other boys she could count on for advice, strength, knowledge, and a funny joke here and there. She smiled.

Maylis and Dagon were slumped in the corner, fast asleep. There was a pretty good chance they weren't going to get up anytime soon. In their defense, they barely had any shut-eye since the boat ride two nights ago. Just looking at the boys peacefully sleeping tempted Aidryan to lie down on the soft velvet cushion and join them. Her head hit the pillow, and her mind went completely blank.

Zennith wasn't entirely sure how they were going to get rid of ten knocked out teenagers. After Dagon, Maylis, and Aidryan flew away, Mr. Gobique waved his wand and made the entire rotten gang fall asleep. Then he took a quick shower to get rid of all the germs. Zennith heard Mr. Gobique coming down the stairs to meet him.

"*Ahh*, that was fun!" Mr. G said.

"Very much so," Zen agreed.

Mr. Gobique took a seat on one of his fancy chairs and motioned for his new apprentice to do the same. "I don't want to start your training until we get rid of these pesky teens."

"Sounds good," Zennith said. He was disappointed that he'd have to wait but happy that Mr. G said *we* instead of *I*. In the back of the room, one teen stirred, giving Mr. G a minor heart attack.

"You know what, I changed my mind. Your training begins now."

Dagon bolted upright. "It was just another dream," he breathed. He moaned slightly and wiped his eyes. He glanced over at his sleeping friends. He missed Zen. Dagon pulled the blanket off and stood up. Maylis was snoring away, unbothered by nightmares. He peeked over at Aidryan. He knew she was the last one to sleep so there was no chance of her being woken and not killing him. No matter how much he needed a friendly voice, he absolutely had to fight the urge. Dreams made him feel like that, vulnerable and weak. He never died in his dreams but he was always in danger. Once he dreamed he was in a tall building, walking up and down various staircases. The entire compound was made out of stairs, and there were no windows or doors. The most unnatural part was when he woke up. The dream was still going on, but he was awake at the same time. Although he was frightened by those types of dreams, he never had the same one twice. Usually, they would occur when he was stressing over an event or the outcome of something in the future.

The strange lighting made Dagon feel like it was early in the morning. Or was it morning? Afternoon? The apocalypse? The carriage was thoroughly enclosed except for a few windows at the front. Dagon craned his neck and looked outside. To his surprise, it was neither light nor dark outside. A hazy pink mist surrounded the carriage.

"Hey, Rarity!" he called out. "What's with the sky? What time is it? Can you see where you're going? Where *are* we going anyway?" The questions flew with forceful speed, and Dagon thought he'd never get made fun of by a magical creature, but the snicker coming from this winged horse proved otherwise.

"Don't get your princely robes in a twist! I can see exactly where we are going. Remember, my vision is greatly superior to your puny senses." And that, ladies and gentlemen, was the first time Dagon, the prince of Lamin, got sassed by a magical creature.

"*Oh! Umm*, sorry."

"What I *don't* know is where you people need to go next." For being an inanimate object just a few days ago, she was very persnickety.

Luckily, Dagon had already memorized the map of their travels so he knew exactly where to go next. "Egypt," he said. "Near the pyramids."

Rarity nodded.

"So what about this hazy mist?" Dagon asked her.

The winged horse made a sharp right, causing Dagon to bump his head on one of the windowsills.

"At the moment, we are passing through Gnith territory."

Dagon wasn't quite sure he heard her right. "Ga—what?"

Rarity explained, "Gnith is the Lord of Confusion. That is most likely why you can't see clearly and have no concept of time. Fortunately for me, he thinks I'm a chaise lounge and doesn't consider me a threat."

Dagon stared at her, dumbfounded, but also slightly impressed. "A chair wouldn't be on my list of threatening things," he agreed, "but I also have another question. How do you know so much about him?"

She seemed a bit annoyed with yet another question but answered anyway. "As soon as I transformed, all of these instincts and knowledge were given to me, along with the ability to communicate with humans. That Aidryan girl used a very powerful spell. You could never have this amount of mind capacity as a simple chair."

"No kidding!" Dagon sounded sarcastic but totally meant it. He headed back to his spot in the beautifully decorated escape pod and warmed himself with a few blankets and some pillows. Although he felt confused, most of the time he was awake, Dagon was actually enjoying the thought of the unknown. For a moment, he was completely relaxed. His eyes became heavier by the growing minute. Long, slow breaths followed.

"Dagon!"

His eyes burst open when his name was suddenly called.

"Dagon, wake your friends!" Rarity urged. "We've got trouble ahead."

25

POTIONS, SPELLS, AND STRENGTH

Zennith's mind was racing. It literally felt like horses were running laps in his brain and a bunch of watery mud was flying everywhere. Here he was in this mansion, on an island unknown to man, surrounded by jungle-like terrain and ten sleeping teens that could wake up at any moment and kill him. "Just my luck," he sighed. On the plus side, he had a trained, dangerous magician at his side if anything happened. In addition to the racehorses in his head, there was excitement up there as well. Maybe he could learn curing spells that could kill harmful bacteria with no side effects. He would be an award-winning young doctor—if he ever got off the island, of course.

Zennith followed Mr. G down a bunch of stairs. After about three minutes of twisting and climbing down levels, they eventually reached the bottom. Zennith's feet seemed to have forgotten how to stand still and balance on a level surface. He took a second to get himself back together before gawking at his new surroundings. The magician's lair looked about what you would expect from a magic-obsessed fanboy. Zen also noticed that Laminian symbols were painted on almost every wall and were even embroidered on some old tapestries. It made him feel like he had a little piece of his friends with him when he looked at the symbols. Lined up along the walls were bookshelves of every shape stuffed full of spell books. Zennith even recognized a few that he read back home when he was a kid. The second thing he noticed was the equipment lined up on many wooden tables. There were test tubes, jars filled with strange contents, and . . . purple cauldrons?

Mr. Gobique's face showed that he was particularly proud of his setup.

"Now, Mr. Zennith, this is where the magic happens! First and foremost, we need to make a quick tonic to get those rude adolescents off my beautiful island."

Zennith smiled when he said *we* again. It really made him feel included and capable.

"We just have to find one that will do the trick," he announced as he paced over to one of the bookcases and ran his finger down the spines. "Floatation, no. Vicious animals, maybe later. Death, no, thanks." Bummed, he trudged to the next book collection. Suddenly, he stopped and his big eyes lit up as he grabbed a book. "I can't believe I didn't think of this before! Oh silly me." He dashed back to Zennith and handed the book to him.

Zen's eyes lit up almost as much Mr. G's. "*Whoa!* There's a potion for erasing memories?" He gawked at the title.

"Of course there is! Now we don't have any more time to waste! You prepare the cauldron and find the safety goggles while I grab some of the other essential ingredients like a plastic covering for my new rug."

Zen looked at him and cocked his head to one side.

"Some of these potions can get a little messy," he explained.

In just a few minutes, both were back with their supplies.

"Okay, Zennith, the first thing any good magician does is assess the situation. For example, we have dangerous people on our property that shouldn't be here. What do we do first?"

"Be aware of the time frame," Zennith answered. "We have no idea how long we have until they wake up."

"Very good! I'm going to prep the potion while you contain them all into one specific spot."

"Got it—wait!" Mr. Gobique turned around to meet his gaze. "Does that mean I have to climb back up all those stairs again?"

Mr. G laughed. "No, of course not! The stairs were just for dramatic effect. I have a working elevator to the right of the stuffed giraffe over there."

"Okay, good," Zen said, relieved. He hopped over to the giraffe and pressed the button that took him up to the teenager-filled room. "Nothing to fear," he told himself as the elevator doors opened in front of him. Fortunately for Zen, all the attackers, including Ty, were accounted for and lying in roughly the same section of the large room. It felt as if he were stepping through an unearthed graveyard. *What would be the best place to store ten sleeping teenagers? What about a huge locked closet?* There was a storeroom roughly twenty feet away. "I guess that will have to do."

One by one Zennith lugged each sleeper by the arms into the hideaway. It made him think of his mother and how she sometimes had to do this with him. He'd watch a TV show and often fall asleep before it was over, so his lovely mom would peel him off the couch and direct him to his bed. After a lot of precious time and muscle aches, he relaxed, knowing that he had only one more person to put into the supply closet. Zennith had purposely saved the ringleader for last, and now the time had come. Ty was about as heavy as the other boys he dragged away, but they hadn't nearly as much muscle. Zen was about five feet away from completing his task when he heard a faint sneeze coming from inside the closet.

26

YET ANOTHER ISLAND

It didn't take long for Dagon to wake his friends up, probably because he didn't stop shaking them and screaming until they did. Plus, the confusion in his brain was making the situation worse and worse by the minute. Dagon watched with pity, frustration, and laugher as his sleepy friends attempted to get ready in a moving vehicle. After a few minutes of unreliable gravity, the carriage went through weather that made even Dagon stumble. He went back up to talk with Rarity to see if she had an update on their current conditions. Then he remembered the Laminian treasure they were transporting.

"Aidryan!" he gasped. "Where is the coin you found? Do you still have it?"

Aidryan looked up from putting her cloak on. "No, I don't, come to think of it," she answered.

"We need to find it." Dagon was doing his very best to stay calm. "It's the most important thing we have right now."

Aidryan nodded and began to dig through all their belongings. While Aidryan and Maylis were searching, Dagon decided they should land soon to prevent any damage to themselves and their ride home.

"Hey, Rarity, is there any chance that we could land softly somewhere with no danger?" Dagon thought about what he said and then changed his mind. "Scratch that. Any chance we can land?"

The pegasus answered, but it was extremely difficult for Dagon to comprehend what she was saying with all the ruckus going on.

"The Lord of Coffee is making this happy. He is in a food with the King of Lamin, your feather, which makes him not lick you much."

Dagon was able to make out the words that mattered and guess the ones in between. The pegasus began her decent. Halfway down, there was a large jolt. The force made Aidryan trip and nearly fall out the door.

"He's too powerful! You'll need to jump. I'll be fine," Rarity urged.

Dagon understood every word this time around. Just like that, the three kids hurtled out the door with hands intertwined as if all that mattered was that they were together. When the detail of the ground below them became more and more discernible, Maylis recited a spell to break their fall. They felt themselves slowing down and were heading for a clearing. They reached the ground with no trouble, but fate decided to extend their anxiety a bit further. Aidryan had a more complex landing than her friends. Her feet tripped over something that made her step backwards. Conveniently, there was a steep hill right behind her. Out of instinct, her arms grabbed on to the nearest solid forms, and gravity took care of the rest. So not only did Aidryan roll down the hill, so did her not-so-fortunate friends.

After the initial shock of falling, rolling down the grassy hill was just a childish adventure. They probably wouldn't have minded the sudden tumbling too much if it weren't for all the dirt and the possible resulting brain damage. Maylis seemed to have the worst experience of all. Like many fun things, it started out innocently. But one wrong move and it gradually corrupted until it took a big chunk of their happiness with it. A few scratches, surprise mud puddles, and painful mini rocks later, Maylis came to a stop face up on the ground, just a few seconds after his friends had stopped spinning, and was hardly able to move. A good amount of recovery time would be required after that. It was actually the first time since they dropped out of the sky that they noticed the odd color looming above them. One poked the other, and pretty soon, they were all gawking at the purple tornado from which they had been spewed.

Aidryan looked back at her awestruck friends. "Okay, well, there is no time to lose. We still need to get to . . " She paused to look at the map. Her gaze followed her fingers to the next spot.

"Egypt," Dagon offered. "Our next location is in Egypt."

Maylis and Aidryan groaned at the thought of traveling all the way to Egypt. It was especially annoying because they were still pretty shaken up from the unexpected landing. Each of them sat on the nearest boulder and took a gander at the new territory. There were palm trees and extremely tall and leafy plants that seemed to soar higher than the birds could fly. Off in the distance, between the trees, they glimpsed crashing waves in all directions. Another island. Since she had visited many wilderness-type places in her life, Aidryan was the calmest of the bunch and was starting to warm up to the idea of going to Egypt. At least she could learn a history lesson there.

Dagon sat down next to his cousin. His eyes darted to the Laminian symbol printed in gold on Aidryan's cloak. That was the exact moment he remembered what one of his main concerns was (keep in mind, he had just rolled down the side of a hill so his memory was a bit slower than usual).

"Aidryan!" he blurted. This outburst nearly caused his cousin to fall off the rock they were sitting on. "Do you have the coin? Did you manage to find it before we jumped?" There was panic in his voice.

"Oh," she said. She dug through her pockets. After ten seconds of frantic rustling, she turned to Dagon with a dejected face. "No, I don't have it."

Dagon took a deep sigh and hung his head.

"Wait a sec, does this count?" In Aidryan's hand was the shiny platinum coin. Although it had been through so much, it still managed to look as sparkly as ever. Even with a messed up mind in a messed up place, Aidryan managed to crack a joke and make light of a crazy situation.

Dagon tilted his head up slightly, unsure of how to react. Was he supposed to be happy that she had it or slap her silly for scaring him like that? Luckily for Aidryan, he went for a big hug and a simple thanks.

"Well, now that you two made up and everything is right with the world, we need to sort out some transportation," Maylis piped up. "I don't think we can count on our winged friend to get us out right away. So does someone have any other bright ideas?"

Every mind was turning to the best of its limited ability, on how to solve this next crisis. The time they spent pondering over their troubles seemed like forever, at least until Dagon remembered (somehow) what Rarity told him right before their unexpected skydive.

"What about the person in charge of this island? Maybe he or she can get us out of here," Dagon remarked.

"Listen, Dags," Maylis spoke gently. "Gnith is not the best person to ask for help. He and your father are not exactly best buddies. They aren't even on the Christmas card level."

"I'm aware of that, but are you sure he would know who I was if I just walked up to him looking like a simple teenager?" Dagon asked.

"But, Dags, did you see the way he cursed the skies when we rode in?" Maylis said calmly. He had grown fond of his ability to make up good nicknames and felt like it helped him connect with others. However, when he attempted this trick with Aidryan, she refused to let him call her Aids—ever!

"I suppose you're right, but I still don't see another option. If we act like we have nothing to hide and not mention our Laminian connections, we could potentially pull this off. No problem."

"Potentially—" Maylis muttered.

"No problem," Aidryan added.

Neither of them seemed convinced of Dagon's plan, especially since they knew more about Lamin's evil creatures than he did.

Dagon crossed his arms. "Come on, guys. This is our only shot. I don't want to be on this island any more than you do. So what do you say? Use our amazing teamwork and dumb luck or become little island men?"

Aidryan cleared her throat loudly.

"And women," he added.

There was more silence and concerned stares, but eventually everyone was on the same page. Packing up their things didn't take very long because they had only one backpack filled with water bottles and a book of emergency quick spells Maylis snagged right before they went plummeting through the sky.

"All right, Maylis. I'm going to let you lead us to the Lord of Confusion because you were *almost* able to get us all out of that museum undetected." Dagon patted Maylis's back and let him go in front of the group.

"Wait!" Aidryan stopped them. "Do you even know where this guy lives? We could be looking for days, especially because our minds aren't exactly dependable at the moment."

Maylis turned to her, slightly put off. "Listen, Aidry," he started, "we have been through much worse. And I'm sure with my knowledge, your good tracking skills, and the legendary prince of Lamin to lead us, we can achieve anything."

Aidryan pondered what her friend said. "Well, okay then. If you are so sure that we won't be dead by tonight, then I trust you," she answered. She stepped right up to his face and looked him dead in the eye without any loss of focus so that Maylis's stomach screamed a little. "However, if we die out here, I am 100 percent blaming you." She stormed off, leaving Maylis and Dagon in the dust.

"Where the heck did you find her?" Maylis asked.

"I have no idea," Dagon answered with a smile.

When the boys finally caught up with the ever confident Aidryan, they began to enjoy their time together. They launched into old stories from training camp when they all first started using the art of magic.

"I have to say, at least this is better than when you nearly turned me into a human campfire when your spell went horribly wrong," Aidryan told Dagon.

"Well, what about the time when you *accidentally* took my voice from me for the entire day?" Dagon added.

"Oh yeah! Best day of my life!" she joked and playfully shoved Dagon into Maylis.

"Yes, those were fun times, but nothing compared to the time when you trapped yourselves inside your tents with powerful magic (that you weren't supposed to know about) and it took you almost five hours to undo it." Maylis commenced his maniacal laugh while the others pushed him down. That, however, didn't stop his giggling.

"Hey, you didn't exactly help out!" Aidryan yelled.

"Yeah, I just heard you laughing and eating all of the chips and salsa my mom made for us," Dagon remarked.

The lively banter went on for a while, which helped with morale and general happiness throughout the group. Nevertheless, when Maylis and the others looked up at the sky that was ominously getting darker, they remembered their task. Maylis exchanged glances with them that signaled they were close. For the next few minutes, they made the atmosphere quiet and simmered in the memories they just discussed. Dagon still couldn't believe

Aidryan was carrying a bucket full of sass with her today. He liked that about her. Whenever someone would say something that she wasn't fond of, she would always have a smart remark that was neither mean nor particularly kind and would leave the person baffled for the whole day. Dagon, come to think of it, had been the recipient of a few of them himself.

Aidryan loved having her cousin with her. She thought this journey made them closer, and it calmed her to know how much he cared. She also admired how calm and collected he was about suddenly becoming a prince. It was just his personality, a trait, that Aidryan wished she possessed. Aidryan admired his easygoing attitude and was glad he was making good use of his leadership talents.

Maylis thought about how lucky he was to have the opportunity to go on his first major quest with some of the funniest people he had ever met. His life in Lamin was happy, but he always wondered what it would be like to live in a world where people had to rely on themselves or each other instead of magic. He almost thought it was a better way to address problems than to just make them magically disappear. Maylis promised himself that he would guide and protect each of his friends until they didn't need his help anymore and maybe a little bit after that.

Dagon was the first to notice that the flowers around them were gradually becoming wilted and frail. In a plentiful place like this, the plants and grass that supported all the wildlife should be healthy. The dying flowers, however, gave him a different opinion. Maylis was talking to Aidryan about the island's host, Gnith. He was impressed to find out how much she already knew about the being and how much she could elaborate. He, of course, added a fact here and there. But Aidryan seemed very informed and passionate about what she was contributing to the conversation, which was why she and Maylis didn't particularly agree with Dagon's plan.

Even Dagon started to have second thoughts when he noticed the flowers. He hated to interrupt their conversation, especially when Aidryan was going off on one of her information rants, but he figured she wouldn't get mad if it were important.

"Maylis? Aidryan?" he asked.

They quickly turned to him, waiting for a worthy question to replace their conversation. "Did you guys notice these flowers? I don't think this is normal plant behavior."

Maylis crouched down next to a small yellow daisy-like plant. He felt the coarse leaves with his fingers. He suddenly had a realization, and he whispered something under his breath. Maylis and Aidryan sat in the same position for longer than was expected, which made Dagon nervous. They both exchanged glances, and Maylis mumbled so quietly that Dagon wasn't able to catch it. Maylis slowly turned toward Dagon. "This flower is frozen, and so are the ones over there." He motioned with his hand behind Dagon. All around them, more and more plants, trees, and even some small animals began to freeze. Aidryan gasped when she saw Maylis's breath clearly. Nevertheless, no matter how cold and frost-covered it got, Dagon, Aidryan, and Maylis themselves weren't cold at all.

Maylis bolted up. "Forget everything you see!" he told his friends. "Think about anything normal. It will help your perplexed brain be less shocked if it sees something extraordinary. The Lord of Confusion knows where we are." Maylis told them to find cover. The three of them dove beneath a fluffy pink tree whose branches were infested with tiny elves singing Taylor Swift songs and sitting in teacups.

"So how exactly do we confront this problem?" Dagon asked.

"I think we have to follow the most bizarre features we see until they lead us to his castle," Maylis answered. "And from the looks of this tree, we are on the right track."

"So we have a plan?" Aidryan asked.

"Our instincts," replied Maylis. He lifted his head to politely ask the elves to stop singing, but when that didn't work, he regained focus on Aidryan who was clearly more annoyed than he was at the performing elves. "Let's just keep going," he suggested. They were about to bolt across the field toward a lion dancing with a three-headed land whale until Maylis remembered something and stopped his friends. "One more thing," he mumbled. "Gnith probably knows that we have the prince with us."

Maylis and Aidryan both looked at Dagon who immediately began rethinking his whole *brilliant* plan. They didn't have much time to think about it because it started snowing at full velocity. Dagon still couldn't get over the fact that he wasn't even cold and that just made him distrust this guy even more.

Dagon, Aidryan, and Maylis ran through the strange woods, following a crooked line from one bizarre plant or creature to the next and saw many things impossible to describe. Each was more peculiar than the last, which made them feel like they must be getting closer to their goal. Aidryan was now in front of the group and was the first to see a sunny clearing about twenty yards ahead.

They arrived at the clearing, panting from exertion. When their vision adjusted to the brightness, the young heroes didn't know whether to laugh or be frightened because sitting atop a large hill was an exact replica of Cinderella's Disney World castle, moat and all.

People usually imagine a villain's lair to be built in a setting that oozes world domination. They expect the evil den to be situated someplace dark, far away from civilization. It would even pass for a lair if it were in an inhospitable place like the top of a mountain or deep underwater. But this? This was the last place any self-respecting super villain or vicious magical creature would call home. The only thing that gave its evil nature away was the large cloud swirling above its lofty turrets. Although it was an attractive shade of princess pink, it undulated menacingly.

The kids were now 100 percent sure they had found the right place. Once they figured that out, the air around them seemed to clear up. Their brains went back to normal. When they turned around, nothing weird was lurking behind them. Dagon turned to Maylis. They exchanged glances that showed they were thinking the same thing: which kiddie ride they should test out first? After their brain function improved, their priorities went back to normal, for better or worse. Both boys raced up the hill toward the castle, shocked to discover Aidryan was already leading the way.

"Hey, wait up, Aidry!" Maylis called.

Aidryan looked back at them with a super wide smile that said, *"If you want me to slow down, then you'll just have to speed up."*

27

MEETING CONFUSION

When he heard the sneeze, Zennith dropped Ty on the ground and ran to hide behind the stairs. Sometimes when he felt scared, he would talk to himself in a quiet manner to calm himself down. Having a bag of chips also didn't hurt. Zennith stood snacking in his hiding place while thinking of escape plans should Ty and the rest of his crazy gang wake up. *Okay*, he thought, *if they wake up, I will either have to run for my life or take on all of them myself.* Zennith gulped, put down the bag of chips, and stepped out of his hiding place. He quickly tiptoed past the sleeping Ty and over to the now threatening supply closet. Then he remembered he was in plain sight and wondered if it had been a good idea to leave behind the comfort of his chips.

"*Achooo!*"

Zennith ran so fast, the Flash himself would have been impressed.

"Maybe it's best if we think of an escape plan just in case our instincts fail us when we get in there," Dagon suggested.

When they finished riding the bumper cars and eating their spicy tacos, they devised a plan on their way to the gate of Gnith's lair (i.e., the princess castle).

"Okay, is everyone clear on the plan?" Maylis nervously questioned.

"Yeah. Go inside, convince the Lord of Confusion not to hate me, set up some sort of transportation, and get the heck out," Dagon enumerated, a bit of sarcasm thrown in for good measure.

There was hardly a difference between the outside of the castle and the inside. There were an abundance of bright-blue curtains with gold and rose-pink designs. Many bushels of flowers adorned the entranceway. Aidryan, Dagon, and Maylis hardly knew where to put their eyes. Everywhere they looked was another girlish embellishment so that even Aidryan, proud female though she was, was embarrassed. Finally, Maylis and the others noticed that the castle was not empty and all their stares were being carefully monitored. There were also two well-dressed guards on either side of the throne holding sharp-looking weapons. They meant business.

Perhaps the most intimidating thing in the room was the being sitting on the throne itself. Gnith wore a bright-red royal coat, which clashed a bit with the castle's décor, but, obviously, caring wasn't on his to-do list today. Dagon was the most intrigued, having very little knowledge of this entity. He was slightly surprised to see Gnith wearing a tailored suit in a variety of gray-and-white shades, which complimented his dark-brown hair and chiseled chin. He almost seemed human—at least human enough to pull off a fancy suit. To top off this classy aspect, a golden crown sat on his head.

For what felt like forever, the companions approached the stylish magical being with steady movements and caution in every step. As planned, they fell into order. Maylis was in the front, Aidryan was to his left and a little behind him, and Dagon was in the back, blocked by the others. Their hope was to avoid as much conflict with Gnith as possible and attempt to make a good impression.

Maylis cleared his throat. "Hello, Sir Gnith, Lord of Confusion. We have come to seek your aid."

"What is your name, boy?" Gnith's voice was so strong and bold, it shook the entire hallway.

"My name is Peter Mothsworthy, and these are my cousins. We are here because we got lost on our way to Lamin, and we were hoping you could help us."

Gnith looked amused at the last statement. "That is very interesting because I sense that you and your friends are not who you claim to be." He smirked. Dagon shifted his weight uneasily. The lord continued, "I'm guessing by the way you are trembling that you know I am someone a person wouldn't normally ask for directions, let's just say that." Gnith let out a small laugh and stood up to his full size, which was roughly eight feet. Even if his choice of abode was a poor fit, he could still send shivers down the Loch Ness monster's lengthy spine. Gnith walked down the carpeted steps until he was face to face with Maylis. He stood on the last step, which gave him an extra foot on Maylis who was already two and a half feet shorter. "You look like the kind of kid who gets pushed around by everyone, even by younger children." He smirked again.

Maylis would have responded but he was too busy thinking of ways to smash the crown so far down on Gnith's stately head that it would become a necklace. He was pretty confident that his friends had the same feelings stirring up inside them too. It was at that moment they realized the Lord of Confusion was a huge egocentric jerk face.

Gnith hardly paid any attention to Aidryan and Dagon before signaling to his guards to detain them. The guards would have had a tough time capturing the companions before the lord's insult, but now the guards had no chance whatsoever. Within seconds Aidryan and Maylis had cornered them with their wands. Dagon, however, stayed behind to face Gnith. He was clearly offended by the way his friend had just been treated. Gnith stared Dagon down.

"Well, if it isn't young Klayric Junior. This certainly is a major turn of events. I sensed you were coming before you entered my domain, and lo and behold, I was right." Gnith removed his red coat and took out his own wand, completely disregarding the fact that his guards were being guarded. "You know, Junior, your daddy is a very bad man for banishing me to a terrible fate, living forever in a castle made for a princess."

"If my dad banished you, he probably had a good reason." Dagon lowered his wand, walked closer, and tilted his head just enough to look into the being's dark stormy eyes. "We expected first class hospitality and some transportation, instead we got insults. Maybe my father should amp up your punishment."

Gnith lost it. A huge wave of fire and rabid bunnies exploded from his wand, but Dagon easily doused the flames, and the bunnies were just a distraction. Aidryan got tired of watching the guards and uttered a spell that glued them both to the ceiling. Their weapons fell uselessly to the floor. As if on cue, more angry guards came flooding into the middle of the throne room and surrounded Aidryan and Maylis. "It's just you and me now, Junior. Just you and me." Gnith took a sword from the wall and set it on fire for dramatic effect.

"You can spray fire and rabbits at me and torment me all you want, but if you touch either of my friends, I will end you!" Dagon yelled. He took a running leap and flew toward Gnith, planting his foot squarely in the lord's chest and knocking him to the floor.

Just then, the glass skylight above the throne shattered. Rarity emerged, carriage and all. She swooped down, sending the guards scattering in all directions. "Did someone order taxi service?"

28

I'm Going to Like It Here

It was extremely unlikely that Ty would be pleased to find his people locked in a closet. So Zennith did the only thing that made sense to his flustered brain. He ran as fast as he could to the safety of Mr. Gobique's lair and its storehouse of magic. When Zennith finally shot out of the elevator, accidentally knocking over the giraffe in the process, a wave of relief washed over him when he saw that Mr. G was already bottling up the potion in mini pink squirt bottles. Magic wands are great, but what is better than *sprayable* magic? Absolutely nothing.

"Ah, Zennith! Did you secure our guests?" he inquired with a boost of enthusiasm.

"*Um*, well," Zennith gasped, "all except one."

"That's nearly everyone so I'd say you are doing wonderfully so far! Why do you look so pale? Not enough sun?"

"I wish that were the case, but I'm actually olive skinned. Turns out we might need that potion a little bit sooner than we would have liked."

Mr. G read Zen's expression and immediately knew what the stakes were. His face turned serious as he handed Zen one of the loaded pink bottles. "Go back up there and fend them off for a while until I finish with these. I'll be quick, don't worry."

Zennith should have been less scared from this reassuring gesture, but he would much rather go into battle with an experienced magician than a plastic bottle. But this was no time for emotions. Zen trotted back to the elevator and politely restored the giraffe to its upright position before entering. After stepping out of the comfort of the lift, he moved ninja-style toward the room where the half-conscious teens were stored. However, what he found there was not what he expected at all. Instead of dazed boys and girls with drool in their hair, he saw quite the opposite. Boys were up and walking around, throwing in some kicks for good measure. Some were fashioning karate *bo* staffs out of the wooden supply closet door. Handfuls were practicing their death stares. The girls were no exception. A few of them sported a full face of makeup as they sharpened their knives. *I hope my friends come to my funeral,* Zennith thought as he stepped into the light. Some noticed his sudden appearance and looked up from their battle preparations. Others stood up abruptly, which made Zennith flinch.

Then Ty made himself known. He walked toward Zen with a smirk on his face. Having no shirt on his torso, his muscles were bulging.

"Well, if it isn't the little sidekick," Ty sneered. Where is your group leader? Dragon, I think you called him."

"*Humph!*" Zennith grunted in response.

"It doesn't look like he's here. Did he abandon you?" Now the others joined in mocking him, sounding more like laugh tracks than actual people.

"Hey, Ty, it looks like you and your buddies are not dealing well with the warm island weather." Zennith held up the bottle so that Ty could see the clear liquid inside the pink-tinted plastic. "This will cool you off."

Before anyone could object, Zennith pressed the trigger, releasing a stream of magic toward the leader. Unfortunately, at that exact moment, Ty decided to wipe away his manly sweat. Typical. The liquid hit his hands but Zennith soon discovered that in order for the potion to work, it had to make contact with the face. The battle had begun. Zennith did his best to spray all the people he saw with the mystery substance. It was actually going quite well until the bottle began running low. Once Ty and some of his *bo*-wielding followers figured this out, they immediately made their approach. Five of them circled around, ready for a final attack. Zennith was expecting his friend to burst through and save him from being pummeled, but, sadly, that didn't happen.

Ty took one more look at Zennith then sent his fist into his stomach. The force made Zen hit the ground with a *thunk*, which made the whole encounter ten times worse. Zennith was down. The fact that he was on the floor was like an open invitation for the group to take their anger out on him. A punch to his arm, a slap to his face, and a sharp kick to his thigh followed swiftly. Zennith tried his best to become invisible, hugging the squirt bottle to his bruised chest.

"EXCUSE ME!" A loud, thunderous voice came from the doorway. "NO ONE HURTS AN ESTEEMED GUEST IN MY HOUSE!" Mr. Gobique roared again, making the whole squad look up and giving Zennith a moment to find his lungs and push them back into his chest. Strapped under Mr. G's cape was a huge barrel of potion with a hose snaking up to a handheld nozzle. "I hope you enjoy this free cooling session courtesy of Gobique Island—if you can remember it, that is."

With that, he let the nozzle loose and a huge blast of potion thoroughly covered every single person. He wanted to make sure it went all the way up their noses.

After it was all said and done, Zennith uncovered his face and surveyed the situation. Then he stared up at his rescuer. "YOU COULD HAVE COME FIVE MINUTES EARLIER!" he yelled.

Mr. G looked at the floor, a little ashamed. He removed his potion blaster and came to help.

Zennith hoisted himself off the floor but grabbed his ribs when he heard a crack. "I think my rib's broken," he grumbled as Mr. G arrived.

"Looks like you're right." He examined Zen's abdomen, face, and arms. "However, another good thing about being a magician is the fact that we never have to wait long to feel better."

Zennith nodded. He limped to a nearby chair. With his remaining strength, he began to think of a healing spell that Maylis had taught him after he got nicked by one of Aidryan's stray arrows. He lifted his hand over himself and closed his eyes for focus. A few seconds later, Zennith felt much better and was ready to stand on his own.

"One problem solved, another one formed," Mr. G said as he looked at all the attackers lying stunned on his floor. "I think the next step is to make sure they never come back . . . *Aha!*" Mr. Gobique got up from where he was sitting and ran into a side room. He came back with what looked like women's clothes. He dropped them on the ground in front of Zennith and inspected his eyes for approval.

"You want me to dress up like a maid?" Zennith asked with obvious confusion and a tiny bit of curiosity in his voice.

"Yes! We have to make it seem like they wound up here because they were lost. We will simply give them crazy directions and hope they end up in Greenland. It's an entirely genius plan."

"Fine. I want them gone as much as you do, so I'm prepared to do whatever it takes."

"I am so pleased." Mr. Gobique handed Zennith the maid's ensemble and a makeup bag. "I'll meet you back here in five minutes. Quickly, before they wake up."

Zennith turned out to be one of the cutest house cleaners ever. He had the stereotypical short black dress with white frilly details and a matching white hat on top of a brunette wig. To top it all off, he had a feather duster, gloves, and subtle makeup on as well.

"We will never speak of this, do you hear me?" Zennith snapped.

Mr. G had on a similar outfit and looked completely ready to get into character. "Of course, this is between you and me only." He let out a small laugh. "*Tee-hee!*"

"Whatever. Are you ready?" Zen asked.

Mr. G gave him the thumbs-up. "Hello, darlings!" Mr. G said in his best girly voice. "Don't be sleeping on the floor now, it's not a very proper way to rest. A bed's the way to go."

Each person groggily stood up and looked around. "Where are we?" one girl asked.

"Here, let me help you. I think you and your lovely friends need some transportation. There is a boat anchored to my dock that will fit you all very nicely." Mr. G held the girl's shoulders and directed her toward the front door. He turned back to Zennith and motioned for him to say something, making it clear that it wasn't an option.

"Oh, yes!" Zen coughed. "The boat will be a very good fit. Come on, everyone, out the door so you can get back home as soon as possible!" *Or wherever you end up*, he thought.

As if they were life-size action figures, each teen, including Ty, stomped out the door toward the boat. Both Zen and Mr. G waved their feather dusters and said repeatedly, "Bye-bye my dears." Mr. G got out a handkerchief and dabbed his eyes for good measure. One of the girls even waved back as Ty started the engine.

Once the boat was just a speck in the distance, Zennith and Mr. Gobique let out a huge breath, threw down their wigs, and pulled off their sweaty gloves. "Well, wasn't that fun?" asked Mr. G.

"Oh yeah, it was wonderful," Zennith said in a high-pitched voice. "We are never doing that again."

"Oh please, it wasn't that horrible."

Mr. G and Zen both laughed.

"I think we should change. This outfit isn't as comfortable as it looked online," Mr. G said as he closed the front door and locked it up tight.

"That's the best idea you've had today," Zennith agreed.

29

EGYPT AT LAST

For someone who had never seen an ancient non-magical civilization, it sure seemed like Maylis knew more about Egypt then any of the well-educated students sitting beside him.

"My parents used to tell me about Egyptian myths and culture when I was a young boy," he explained. "They told me how Lamin often set up trade agreements with the world below and that some of the ancient pyramids are actually Laminian owned."

Aidryan turned to Maylis. "So do you think we will find our next piece of treasure in one of the Laminian-owned pyramids?"

He looked back at her. "I don't have any doubt in my mind."

As the carriage flew lower, each person took huge gasps and displayed their admiration and curiosity for the unfamiliar land. None of the travelers had been there before, but they could definitely see it lived up to its reputation. Rarity had been careful to stay out of sight until she was able to pull the carriage to a small Laminian outpost. She barely touched the ground before all three companions tumbled onto the hot coarse sand.

SOPHIA BORZILLERI

Aidryan stood and dusted herself off. Since their escape from the vengeful teens, the young heroes had not changed clothes or taken a shower. The carriage didn't smell like it did a few days ago, to say the least, and Aidryan was on a mission to change that. For a little over an hour, she hunted for a place that would give them just that. Dozens of tent shop owners were hawking water and souvenirs. Unfortunately for her, she was slowed down by the fact that she could not speak the native language, let alone understand it, so many of the conversations were over in mere moments. When she finally accepted failure, she found the nearest rock, sat down, and sulked in the sun like an annoyed snake. This gave Maylis and Dagon time to find her since she had thunderously taken off before either of them could get a word out.

"Oh, thank you for finally stopping. I almost got heatstroke chasing after you," Maylis expressed his annoyance toward her actions.

"I'm just trying to get us cleaned up and out of these disgusting clothes!" Aidryan snapped.

"All right, you two. Let's look for assistance together. I know that Maylis is very familiar with Egyptian customs and can even speak a little of the native dialect," Dagon reasoned.

Aidryan looked up at Dagon and narrowed her eyes. "Well, don't give him all the credit! I can offer plenty of skills that can help us, including—"

Dagon cut her off. "And Aidryan can contribute mad people skills and remarkable pleasantness."

Aidryan gave Dagon a look, but he could tell that she was satisfied with the way he described her character. He held out his hand to her and helped her stand back on her own two feet. She politely smiled but remained at the back of the party, clearly not in the mood for any more conversation until she was clean. The kids made their way back through the line of vendors, now with someone who could carry on a somewhat successful conversation. They didn't have to travel far before Maylis found someone who directed them to a small hotel just a few blocks away. The hotel had a sign plastered on one of its sides that Maylis translated into "cold water, delicious food, and gift shop." That was good enough for a devastatingly tired girl like Aidryan. After her satisfying shower, she came out of the bathroom wearing the hotel's expensive-looking white robe.

"*Ahhh!* Isn't this great? I actually feel like talking to you two again."

Maylis grunted, "Well, it would be a lot greater if you hadn't hogged the shower for thirty minutes while the rest of us had to wait in our own mire."

Once they were properly cleaned, dressed, and fed, they decided to tour their location. For the rest of the day, they explored the different shopping areas and ancient ruins while wearing their new Egyptian clothes. They even ran into someone who was performing magic and asked Aidryan to be a volunteer. She accepted instantly and even showed off some tame magic herself.

Maylis piped up, "I guess things worked out well between our two cultures since there is magic being performed in the streets. If that doesn't scream peace, I don't know what does."

Toward the end of the day, when the light in the sky turned reddish and dim, the gang returned to their hotel. Aidryan found a patio in the back of the building that offered a beautiful view of the distant pyramids.

"You were right, as usual, Aidryan. This is a great view," Maylis admitted.

Aidryan gave Maylis an apologetic smile and wrapped her arms around him, embracing him in a tight hug. Shortly after, she pulled Dagon in as well.

Bright and early the next morning, Dagon, Aidryan, and Maylis went to visit Rarity. They were happy to see that someone was already taking care of her. When the pegasus saw them coming, she lifted her head from her water trough and whinnied with glee.

"I'm so happy you're back! I see you have settled in quite nicely," she said.

The kind stable hand that was tending to her proved he was of Laminian descent because he was completely unfazed when the winged horse began speaking in full sentences. He looked up from what he was doing, bowed his head toward the kids, and went off to attend to other animals. Dagon acknowledged him and bowed back in a respectful manner.

"That man was very kind to take care of you like this. When I am king, I will make sure he is rewarded," Dagon declared.

"I think that would be a splend—" Rarity was only able to get out half a sentence before someone started yelling over a loudspeaker and caught their attention. Neither Dagon nor Aidryan had any idea what the man was saying until Maylis whispered a spell quietly under his breath. Moments later, both Aidryan and Dagon could understand and speak the language perfectly.

"That spell would have been useful yesterday," she mumbled and playfully nudged Maylis in the ribs.

"Listen, all of you!" the loudspeaker man shouted. "There is a tour bus leaving at 8:00 a.m. tomorrow for the pyramids of Lamin. Get your tickets now!"

"I guess it's all settled then." Maylis laughed when he saw Dagon speed walk through a group of villagers and make a beeline for the ticket booth.

"There's one problem though," Aidryan began. "If any word is said about Dagon being the prince, things might happen that could take us off course. I don't think anyone would try to hurt him like Gnith, but I just couldn't live with myself if something happened."

Maylis nodded in agreement. "Good point. Instead of taking the bus, we will ask Rarity to get us there before dawn."

30

TRAPPED

Waking up early the next morning was extremely difficult for the friends, even though the burning sun gladly assisted by streaming into their eyes.

"I'm really missing my Buzz Lightyear alarm clock right about now," Dagon groaned and sat up.

Aidryan peeked her head around the bathroom door. "You still have that Buzz Lightyear alarm clock? I thought you threw it away a while ago."

"I . . . I had trouble letting it go," he explained.

"Of course you did."

"Will you guys stop bantering and get ready, we have treasure to find," Maylis snapped. He was already dressed with his teeth brushed. He even styled his long hair so that the front half of it was pulled up away from his face.

"Fine," Aidryan said. She did a double take at Maylis, who was looking in the mirror, and realized something. "Is that my hair tie?"

Maylis froze. "Nope. It came with the room." He turned and gave her a guilty smirk.

"*Ugh*, whatever!" she scoffed.

Not long after, Dagon, Aidryan, and Maylis left the comfort of the hotel and started heading in the direction of their winged transportation. Rarity was awake and already hooked up to her carriage by the same man who cared for her when they arrived.

"All right, young heroes, are you ready for another adventure?" Rarity joyfully inquired.

"Wouldn't miss it!" Dagon nodded while Aidryan and Maylis flashed her a warm smile.

"Well, then, let's get going!"

The three companions and the talking pegasus took off toward the pyramids.

The night before Maylis had snatched one of the maps the tour bus was using. He had become quite an expert at taking maps out from under people's noses. He pulled both maps out of his bag and studied them carefully.

"Well, would you look at that," he said. "Doesn't it seem like this could attach right to . . " he trailed off, laid the two map pieces together, and confirmed they fit together perfectly. "This is a very good sign," he noted as Aidryan and Dagon remained shell-shocked.

Without saying a word, Aidryan grabbed both map pieces from Maylis's grip—careful not to rip them, of course—and set them down on the floor of the moving carriage. She closed her eyes, held her hands over them, and whispered an incantation. Soon after, the pieces melded together.

"That should help a bit," Dagon stated.

"Yeah, a bit," Aidryan responded.

"Hey, look outside, you two. We're here!" Maylis called and stuck his head out the window like a happy dog.

After unhitching from the carriage, Rarity spread her wings and flew off. They watched her go. Aidryan envied her ability to literally fly away from her problems without even thinking twice. She was also a tad jealous of the pegasus's bravery. After all, Rarity put herself in danger twice now just to help them escape. Aidryan frowned. *Is it weird that I'm jealous of a horse? And is it even weirder that I'm jealous of something I created?*

"Aidryan!"

"*Whoa!* What?" She flinched and came back to reality.

"We are walking now," Dagon said as he motioned with his hand toward Maylis who was already halfway to the entrance.

"Oh, right, sorry," she mumbled. Aidryan ran to catch up to Maylis, leaving Dagon behind. She didn't want to see his concerned face looking at her.

A few more steps, and they would be closer to finding the second treasure of their journey and one step closer to going home. While Maylis handed out headlamps, Dagon pointed his wand at the many locks. Each clinked open.

"Do you think there will be scorpions in here?" Aidryan asked when they were inside.

"Most likely. They are very common in places like this," Maylis answered without looking up from the map.

Aidryan gave a horrified look and stayed very close to Maylis after getting the disturbing news.

"Look for clues. I don't think the ancient people of Lamin would have hidden a valuable treasure in the center of a lit room," Maylis suggested.

"Okay, let's split up," Dagon piped up from behind them.

Aidryan's throat closed up. "Wait, are you serious?"

"*Um*, yeah, I am. Why? Are you scared?"

"Of course not! I'll take this way," she snapped, avoiding any possible eye contact from either of her friends and hurried off in that direction.

By the time Aidryan stormed around the corner, Maylis was moving just as fast in the opposite direction. They had left Dagon alone inside an ancient tomb that was potentially home to a bunch of scorpions. *Okay, maybe splitting up wasn't such a good idea,* he thought.

Maylis's eyes were glued to the map as if it would physically hurt him to peel them from it. He had almost completed translating the map when he suddenly stopped. His mind drifted back to the island where they met Mr. Gobique, and he remembered his run-in with the tree. His face flushed a bright red. He cleared his throat, shoved the map into his pocket, and took out his wand instead. That was when he saw it. There on one of the sealed doors was the main Laminian symbol. It was the biggest one he had seen on their quest so far. He figured if that wasn't a sign sent from above, then nothing was. Cautiously, he approached the door with his wand shoved against the palm of his hand. *Magic's the key*, he thought. Maylis waved his wand in front of the mysterious door, and sure enough, it creaked open. "Easy," he murmured.

Creeping inside, he checked his surroundings for safety and paced farther and farther away from the entrance. He stood in the very center of the room and stared all around. The ceilings were high enough to contain marvelous marble statues of the past rulers of Lamin. Golden treasure lined the edges of the room, and there was a glowing light coming from the far left wall. Using his wand, Maylis lit the rest of the room by making flames erupt from the torches anchored on the walls. It reminded him of the first time Zennith lit an arrow on fire and hit a bull's-eye. Maylis's mood instantly lifted.

It was at that moment that the coin made itself known. There across the sandy stone floor, resting atop a regal pedestal, was the second Laminian treasure. Maylis sprinted toward it at full velocity, slowing down just enough to avoid hitting the pedestal. Knocking an enchanted coin onto the floor could not, in any culture, be a good omen. Ever so delicately, Maylis lifted the coin off its stand and held the precious platinum in the palm of his hands. He turned it over, and sure enough, the Laminian letter *A* was clearly embossed. He began strolling back to the entrance to find his friends and show them what he found (i.e., rub it in their faces). Sadly, the fact that Maylis didn't knock over the pedestal did nothing to boost his good luck factor.

He heard a click. Soon after, his foot began to sink. "Uh-oh!" he said, knowing that every outcome would be bad or worse. The room rumbled and shook, sending Maylis to the floor. He looked up toward the door. It was difficult to see through his long locks (the hair tie obviously wasn't doing its job), but he was sure the door was starting to close. Fear struck and made him do the only thing he could think of. He chucked the coin across the floor and out the door where it skidded into a small pile of rocks.

"Maylis! Oh my gosh, Maylis, are you okay?" Aidryan was calling his name. The worry in her voice was evident. She and Dagon heard the commotion and ran to Maylis's aid as soon as they could. Aidryan rounded a corner and almost whipped down another corridor, but before she could do that, she saw a shimmering light coming from behind a bunch of random rocks. "Dagon, come over here! I think I found the coin," she stated, a bit confused as to why it was in a place like this.

"Really? That's gre—why is it on the dirty floor?"

"That's what I thought."

A groan came from behind the closed door. "Maybe it's because Maylis, your fearless coach, slid it under the door before it closed on it too."

"Aw, buddy, sorry you got locked in. Did something scare you?" Dagon teased.

"Of course not," Maylis defended himself from behind the sealed door. "Just get me out."

"Wait, I think I hear something," Aidryan cut in.

They all went silent and soon found out that Aidryan was right. Voices traveled down the halls and were coming closer.

"Maybe this is a good thing," Dagon reasoned.

Aidryan gave him a look. "Why the heck is this a *good* thing? People could find us here and get suspicious."

"Maybe, but I know they wouldn't hesitate to save a helpless little kid."

"I'm right here, guys," Maylis groaned.

Dagon disregarded his friend and dashed down the hall, looking for help. Aidryan huffed, clearly annoyed, but she charged after him.

"You guys really know how to help a person," Maylis sarcastically joked. He hadn't gotten up since the room began to have a seizure and was secretly hoping it took his friends a while to get help so he could enjoy not moving for a little longer. Dagon and Aidryan came back earlier than Maylis would have liked, but he was still glad to get out of there since the torches were almost out.

"We're here, Maylis!" Aidryan called to him.

"Yeah, don't worry, buddy. We got someone who can help you. I believe you might even know him," Dagon declared.

This intrigued Maylis enough to stand up and lean against a pole in preparation. He heard a man's voice but couldn't quite make out his exact words. His only guess was that he was chanting a spell. Crash! The once sealed door crumpled into tiny bits all over the sandy floor. The dust settled, and Maylis could finally make out a face. "Uncle Maurice?" he asked.

"That's right, my boy. It's wonderful to see you." His uncle was a shortish man with a mustache and dark hair (the same color as Maylis) and a bright smile. He was dressed in a washed-out purple shirt with beige pants and sandals.

Maylis ran toward the man and embraced him tightly. "Uncle, I'm so glad to see you too! What are you doing here?" Maylis began asking him numerous questions.

His uncle did his very best to thoroughly answer each one. He put his arm around Maylis and led him down the hall. Aidryan grabbed the coin off the ground, brushed some of the sand off, and put it in her bag. Maurice asked Maylis if he wanted to ride back with him on his camels. "They are not ordinary camels." He winked.

Maylis immediately agreed. He said a short good-bye to his friends and climbed aboard. Dagon called for Rarity. Soon, everyone was heading back. When they met back at the hotel, Maylis had some unexpected news for Aidryan and Dagon.

"I've been thinking, maybe it wouldn't be so bad if I just stayed with my uncle for a while. I haven't seen him since I was in elementary school, and reconnecting with him would be so nice. I know it's a little sudden but I don't want to miss an opportunity like this. Anyway, both of you have been doing so well that I know you don't really need me anymore . . " he trailed off.

"Of course we still need you," Aidryan said softly. "But we will be fine on our own if you want to stay with your uncle and catch up."

"I totally agree," Dagon piped up.

Maylis smiled at his friends' support and embraced them both. Apparently, he was in a hugging mood that day. Aidryan and Dagon both laughed. Maylis stopped them. "Wait, one more thing, I want to see both of them before I go."

Aidryan understood what he was referring to and took out both coins. "Here they are." She had one in each hand and held them out to Maylis. Distinctly written on each one were the Laminian letters, *L* and *A*. "Three more to go," Aidryan announced.

"Three more to go," echoed Maylis.

31

A Lowly Peasant

The group of four heroes was now down to two. Back in the flying carriage, Aidryan and Dagon began to doubt themselves and the journey ahead. Half the members had followed new paths. Dagon and Aidryan were happy for their friends, but the uncertainty of their own destinies was unnerving.

"Hey!" Dagon nudged Aidryan who was lost in thought with her head out the window. "What if we try to contact Zen and Maylis? Maybe we can check in and see if everything is all right with them."

Dagon knew that Aidryan missed their other companions. She never did well with good-byes, especially when she didn't know the next time she would see them again. Dagon was in a despairing mood as well but he was able to mask it better. Aidryan turned toward him with a blank, melancholy expression on her face. "How could we do that?" she asked. "I have all four of the cell phone books."

Dagon rotated his body to face hers and drew his wand from his pocket. "I know a spell that lets us appear to anyone in the world."

"Really?" Aidryan's spirit lifted just enough to show a bit of her usual pluck.

"Watch, it's really easy. Let's check on Zennith first." Dagon pivoted to face a mirror that was placed toward the front of the carriage. He concentrated, and soon after, light-blue smoke encircled it until an image materialized inside.

Aidryan's smile brightened when she saw Zennith and Mr. Gobique. "Zennith! Mr. G! It's Aidryan, how are you?"

Zen looked immediately up from the cauldron he was gazing into, pulled his goggles off, and laughed when he saw her face. "Aidryan? *Whoa*, that's so cool! Thanks for checking in. I'm fine, by the way," he responded.

"Oh, that's great! It looks like you've been busy."

"Like a bee."

"The only difference between you and a bee is that you can't fly."

"I thought you were going to say that I don't have a harmful backside!"

"Well . . "

"*Hey!* That's mean, Aidryan."

For almost an hour, Aidryan and Zen went back and forth, catching up on everything that had happened since they'd parted (with a few comments thrown in from Dagon and Mr. G). Seeing Aidryan laugh until her stomach hurt when Zen told her about how he and Mr. G dressed up as housemaids made Dagon feel like a good cousin and a loving friend. Zennith was sad to hear that Maylis had also left the group but was still happy for him. He was also a little jealous that he didn't get to go to Egypt but played it off nonchalantly of course. When the meeting came to a close and everyone said their good-byes, Aidryan's mood was back to normal, and the hole in her heart was mended. Dagon made another blue smoke cloud. This time, it popped up in the Laminian settlement in Egypt.

"Hey, Maylie!" Aidryan teased.

Maylis was startled when Aidryan and Dagon's faces suddenly appeared in the well he was standing near, but as he was accustomed to all things magical, it didn't take him long to figure out what was happening. "Well, if it isn't our very own Aids."

"Okay, it has been discussed that *that* name is off limits."

"Yeah, well, how exactly will you stop me?"

"Oh, I'll find a way."

Dagon and Aidryan told Maylis the story about Zennith's costume change, which took a while considering they were laughing more than telling the story. They had a great time catching up until it was time to go.

"Talk to you soon, Maylie!" Aidryan called. She gave Dagon a huge hug and expressed her thanks. A few hours after the calls, Rarity whinnied vigorously to wake the sleepy travelers. Aidryan was the first to gain consciousness and check out what the pegasus wanted them to see. Aidryan saw a heartwarming surprise. Off in the distance, she could see what looked like a village filled with houses and shops. It didn't seem too strange to her at first until she realized that it was literally sitting on clouds. "Dagon, wake up!" Aidryan found the nearest pillow and started whacking his head with it.

"All right, all right! Let my brain adjust before you start pounding it with worry," Dagon grumbled. "Literally," he whispered under his breath. He clambered off his comfortable sleeping place, stuck his head out the window, and gasped. They finally made it to Lamin!

For the next few minutes, he and his cousin danced around the cramped space and sang every song that popped into their minds. Before they could break the carriage with their boisterous stomping, Rarity explained to them that what they were seeing was not the main city of Lamin, but one of its many remote outposts. Rarity landed at a nearby port, which looked a lot like a helicopter pad, and instructed the eager teens to look for items they could use on the rest of their journey. They set Rarity free from the harness and went to explore the village. This particular part of Lamin seemed like any other small town, except for the fact that the shop names and signs were in the ancient Laminian language. Dagon and Aidryan were not well versed in Laminish, and Maylis wasn't there to perform his cool language spell like he'd done in Egypt. However, over the last few months, Maylis had taught them a few key words that helped them connect some meanings. The two companions also found out the hard way that getting too close to the edge of the city limit could result in some of your food going on a free skydiving lesson. After they'd wandered around for a bit, they decided to camp out with Rarity near the carriage landing pad. Dagon sat on the carriage steps while Aidryan sulked inside like a vampire. She was sour at Dagon for bumping her so hard her still warm sticky bun fell off the village, but she realized they'd have to make up now because she had just uncovered some crucial information.

"Hey, you might want to look at this," she muttered without making full eye contact. "Looks like it was no coincidence we stopped here."

Dagon carefully accepted the map, waiting for the alligator jaws to snap, but they never did. He drew his finger across each location they'd already been to. "I thought we were going to the mountains next. Rarity, do you know what happened to the map?"

She trotted over to him. "From what I can see, this location has been magically added. It seems that someone wanted you to come here first."

Dagon, Rarity, and Aidryan all exchanged confused looks. Aidryan stuffed the map back in her bag and looked around to see if she could resolve the mystery.

"Looks like you got my note." Both young wizards turned around with ready wands, an instinct that was now hardwired into their brains. "Please, I mean you no harm. I just want to speak peacefully with both of you." Standing in front of them stood one of the villagers. His clothes were ragged and dull. It matched his scraggly beard and wrinkled skin. In his left hand was the sticky bun Aidryan had lost over the side. He didn't seem like a person who would do any damage so Aidryan and Dagon both lowered their wands and cautiously approached him.

"Hello," Aidryan murmured in a soft tone. "So it looks like you found my sticky bun, and I'm also guessing that you were the one who brought us on this little detour."

The old man nodded. "I heard that you were searching for platinum coins. Is that right, miss?"

"Well, yes—" she began but got cut off.

"Then I have something for you!" He brightened up and tossed the bun to Dagon, who quickly shoved it into Rarity's mouth for safekeeping. The man took Aidryan's hand and walked back toward the village. Dagon could hardly keep up with the guy. Every time he rounded a corner, all he could see was a glimpse of Aidryan's cloak whipping around another. Dagon finally found them in what appeared to be the old man's shop. The man waved a hand at Dagon, motioning for him to come in. Aidryan gave him a nod of approval. The inside of the shop indicated an unhealthy obsession for bizarre objects. No judgment, though. Dagon sat down next to Aidryan and across from their host. There was a small box in the center of the table between them. Dagon took a closer look and almost screamed when he saw how familiar it was. It was identical to the small black box with the Laminian symbol that each of the three heroes received at the very beginning of their quest.

"Would you like to take a look, my boy?" the peasant questioned, clearly seeing yearning on Dagon's face. Without another word, Dagon pulled the box toward him and clicked it open.

Aidryan's smile brightened with each passing second. "Looks like we got a freebie," she said.

Dagon shared her smile and lifted the coin with a Laminian *M* pressed into the pure platinum. "Thank you so much! But how did you know what we were hunting for?"

"That's not important, my boy. Please take this treasure and go safely on your way." Dagon and Aidryan said one more thank you to the old man, then got up to leave. The shopkeeper grabbed Dagon's wrist and looked him in the eye. "Just remember, love is more important than all the treasure in the world."

When they returned to Rarity and the carriage, they triple-checked the map. Sure enough, the outpost had disappeared from the map as though it had never been there in the first place. Dagon and Aidryan took one more look around to engrave all the town's details into their memory. As they entered the carriage, Dagon pried the sticky bun out of Rarity's muzzle, handed it to Aidryan, and offered her a sincere apology. "I'm sorry I knocked the sticky bun out of your hands, Aidryan," he said.

"Thank you," she answered, taking the bun.

"I swear I didn't mean for it to fall all the way off the cloud. I mean, I'm not used to having a five thousand foot drop on every side of me," he added.

Aidryan acknowledged him and went inside to enjoy her treat as Dagon called out the coordinates for their next destination. "All right, Rarity. Looks like we might need to make you a coat with wing holes because it's going to get cold," Dagon declared.

32

STEP RIGHT UP

Living at the Laminian outpost in Egypt was a bit different than growing up in Lamin itself. Instead of shoving the laundry in a machine for forty minutes, Maylis had to manually wash every piece of clothing. The dryer was a clothesline. Nevertheless, Maylis's surging optimism helped him adjust swiftly to his austere surroundings. Living with his uncle made the entire experience a lot more doable. It had been nearly a week since his friends' emotional departure. Maylis's thoughts lingered on them nearly all the time. In fact, it had become so consuming that the other day Uncle Maurice barely saved Maylis from drinking a glass of spicy vinegar that happened to be sitting next to the milk. Maurice knew then that something needed to be done.

The next morning, before the burning sun made its daily rounds, Maurice's brain granted him a wonderful idea. When Maylis finally made it out of bed, Maurice was already downstairs, ready to express his eureka moment. "Maylis, dear nephew, how was your sleep?" Maurice asked innocently.

"It was pretty good, Uncle. Thanks for asking," Maylis responded while pouring himself a (non-vinegar filled) glass of milk.

Maurice got up from the wooden table and looked straight into Maylis's eyes. "It has come to my attention that you miss your friends. It is completely understandable, but I hate to see you like this."

Maylis sighed, "Yes, that's true. But I still want to stay here, Uncle." He hung his head.

"Don't worry, nephew. I have come up with an idea that might help you." Maurice placed his hands on each of Maylis's shoulders. "Instead of staying home and moping around all day, why don't you come work with me at my shop?"

Instantly, Maylis's face lit up. "I would love that! Thank you so much, Uncle!" Maylis ran to his room to change out of his cloud pajamas while Maurice just laughed and laughed.

"All right, Maylis. Your job for today is to man the cashier's spot behind the counter, got it?" Maurice said as soon as they entered the tiny magic shop.

"Completely. I won't let you down." Maylis secretly always wanted to own a shop, especially if magic were involved. Uncle Maurice went out and stood on the sidewalk, calling out to the passersby and tempting them to buy potion ingredients and spell books.

Ding! Ding!

The bell hanging on the door handle disrupted Maylis's reverie. An old woman hobbled in and stalked the shelves, apparently looking for a specific item. Maylis realized this was his chance to make a good impression on his new neighbors.

"Excuse me, young man, but do you happen to have any frog tongues? I have been looking so long and haven't had any luck," the lady said.

Maylis slid his finger down the *F* column on the inventory list. "Looks like they are in aisle four at the very back of the store to the left," Maylis told her.

"Thank you, dear," she said, turning slowly to make her way to aisle four.

It appeared she was struggling to walk, so out of instinct, Maylis used his magic to summon a jar of frog tongues. It flew through the air to his outstretched hand. He handed her the jar with a smile.

"Thank you!" Her face showed genuine gratitude toward the young wizard.

Throughout the day Uncle Maurice would entice customers inside the store, then Maylis would use his magic to summon the item the person requested. Soon people in the small village were talking about the young wizard that made their shopping a little less stressful. Maurice got wind of the news and ran into the store to give Maylis a huge hug. Maurice explained that not many people in this particular village had the power to use magic. They knew it was real but were unable to do it themselves. Some people could manage a few simple enchantments with the use of certain potions but were really quite limited. Maurice was so pleased with Maylis's work that he offered him a permanent job at the shop.

Maylis was extremely grateful for the opportunity *and* for the spell that let him understand and speak the language. Day after day Maylis served each customer with the help of his magical gifts and made so many people happy, including his uncle Maurice. Even when he wandered the streets on his break, people would recognize Maylis and wave. He would give them a toothy smile before strolling on. Maylis was very joyful at the chance to use his unique gift for the good of so many others, but something kept holding him back. It took a while for him to figure out what was keeping him up at night and making things a bit difficult. He thought getting a job would distract him from thinking about his friends—and it did for a time—but gradually, the dismal emotions came flooding back. Dagon and Aidryan were probably doing just fine without him, but he missed them terribly.

Uncle Maurice noticed Maylis's declining mood and wanted to talk to him about it, but it was hard because if Maylis wasn't working or eating, he was sleeping. One day Maylis happened to be sitting on the couch and reading about ancient Egyptian customs. Uncle Maurice came and sat down on the chair across from him.

"Maylis, dear nephew, how have you been recently? I've noticed some sadness in your eyes. Are you all right?"

Maylis put his book down and sighed. "It's my friends, Uncle. I just don't know what to do! I love working at the store, but I still feel like I should be with them."

"Yes, that is very conflicting," Maurice agreed.

They sat in silence for a while, just listening to the fan whir. Then Uncle Maurice had an idea. "You just wait here, I'll be right back," he said. A little while later, Uncle Maurice returned with a surprising guest. As soon as Maylis saw her, he stood right up. "Maylis, I'm sure you know who this is," Uncle Maurice exclaimed.

The old lady from the shop the very first time Maylis had worked there was now standing in the middle of their living room. She greeted Maylis and took a seat on a chair with the help of Maurice.

"Your uncle tells me you aren't very happy these days. He also told me about your friends and the predicament that you are facing. Listen, dear, our life is full of many choices and some are not easy to make. Trust me, I know."

Maylis listened intently to the woman, hoping to catch something that would help him.

"Now I can't make this decision for you, but I do want to say this: go with what is *most* important to you. Both might seem equally important, but there is always one that outweighs the other. You just need to figure out which one that is. I've been alive a little longer than you. This is what I've learned. Do with it what you will."

"Thank you." Maylis smiled.

"You help me. I help you, dear."

The kind lady left, and Maylis was alone with his uncle once again.

"So have you figured out what you want to do?" asked Uncle Maurice.

"I believe I have."

33

AN EXPLOSIVE RESCUE

"Dagon, you are *not* helping me right now!" Aidryan's voice rang through the snow-covered mountains where they had been met by a pair of unfriendly and unhygienic trolls.

"I'm sorry, cuz, but I'm a bit preoccupied at the moment. Why don't you just whip up another pegasus or something?" Dagon snapped back sarcastically just as an angry troll cuffed him on the cheek.

The first few minutes at their new destination hadn't gone as planned. It started when Rarity was forced to land in a misty spot where the view was blocked by falling snowflakes and forceful winds. Then Aidryan and Dagon were surprised to discover two angry shapes surging toward them, wielding terrifying weapons. The harsh weather and hostile hosts were taking a toll on the cousins' moods at a very quick rate. Aidryan was so annoyed at Dagon's last remark that she dropped her sword, turned, and walked away from the troll she was fighting and flicked Dagon on the head. Big mistake.

First of all, the troll she was battling was irritated that she had rudely walked away and second, he didn't like the way she deliberately hurt her companion. He stepped forward and took a huge whack at her head with his heavy wooden club. Aidryan was knocked out cold. Dagon immediately rushed to her. His cheek was still throbbing in pain, but he was mostly concerned about Aidryan at this point. Then something happened. First, he saw both trolls turn and run in the opposite direction. Then he heard a loud *KA-BOOM!* A gust of snow, smoke, and ice came flooding toward him. He instinctively ducked down to cover Aidryan and waited for the residue of the unforeseen eruption to clear.

"WHOA! Did you guys see that? I like totally saved you from Bill and Gerald. I told them not to scare visitors away, but their memories are not what they used to be."

Through the smoke, Dagon looked up to see a human shadow jumping up and down excitedly. Dagon coughed. "Thanks for saving us! I'm Dagon, and this is Aidryan. We traveled here on a quest, which we should really get back to."

The boy laughed. "Good luck getting *her* off the ground and finding a safe place to stay *and* food and water *and* protection from the trolls who *will* come back shortly."

Dagon sighed because he knew what he was about to ask of this boy and already didn't like the outcome. "Would you mind showing us a safe place to stay?"

"Of course, man. But first, let me help you out with your unconscious friend here. She doesn't look too good. I know just the thing to bring her color back. Follow me!"

Dagon didn't want to seem needy for this boy's help, but he was quite anxious to get out of the cold. He knew it would be difficult to drag Aidryan anywhere on his own. His dropping body temperature won him over. "Thanks," Dagon mumbled.

"My name's Chase, by the way," the boy said.

Chase waited until Dagon grabbed Aidryan's ankles before he gently lifted Aidryan's arms and speed walked faster than Dagon had ever seen someone go. He was a man on a mission. Chase was a blond-haired boy and slightly taller than Dagon (Dagon would argue that Chase's fluffy hood gave the appearance of an extra few inches). His eyes were the color of the Florida sky, which softened his fierce features. Dagon couldn't help but appreciate his unstoppable optimism and vigorous attitude.

"We're almost to my house, man!" Chase reassured. He pointed to the side of a rather large hill with a makeshift doorway. In the process of pulling Aidryan's inert body up the incline, the boy lost his footing and fell, taking Dagon and his unconscious cousin on an involuntarily sled ride back to where they started. Chase played it off as a fun little joke as if he intended to scare Dagon half to death. Aidryan would have been impressed but she didn't know it then. He led them inside, helped get Aidryan propped up on a handmade chair and covered her with a knitted blanket. Dagon took one more look at his sleeping cousin before analyzing his surroundings. Chase may have lived inside a rocky hill, but it was astounding how he managed to make it a homey, comfortable place in such an extreme environment. Chase noticed his expression and quickly explained.

"Do you like it, man? I found it ten years ago, and I've been adding to it ever since. It's not much, but it does the job."

Dagon had a perfectly reasonable response ready when a groggy voice coming from the nearby chair interrupted him.

"*Wow!* This is such an adorable home. Are we in Narnia?" Aidryan questioned, sounding sweetly nerdy.

"*Ahaha!* No, this is just my home." Chase chuckled and walked over to help Aidryan out of her chair. She soon realized how ridiculous she sounded. The redness in her face showed her embarrassment. "I'm Chase," he said as he extended an arm. "We would have met sooner, but you couldn't see or hear me."

"Yes, well, it is nice to meet you, Chase. I'm Aidryan," she answered and shook his hand, not taking her eyes off his face. "Thanks for getting me to safety."

Dagon was watching the whole interaction from afar and wasn't quite sure what was happening. *Why was she being so nice to him? She was never this polite to anyone*, he thought. Then a light bulb went off in his brain. *Oh no! Does she like this guy? This is abso-*

lutely absurd. She barely even knows him! While Dagon was thinking this, Chase and Aidryan had begun a newfound friendship. Chase had given her a warm drink, and she was sipping it happily.

"Hey, Dag! Come over here and sit down. Chase was about to tell me his amazing story." She motioned for Dagon to take a seat next to her. Dagon reluctantly left his cozy spot next to the fire and joined Aidryan and her new crush.

Chase began, "This is kind of a sob story, so for those in this room who get emotional, be warned. My parents wanted to visit this place to research a few of the animal species here, being die-hard biologists and all. So they packed up and took me, their only child, to these mountains. And, man, was it cold! Imagine being only seven years old and taken to a place with no friends or any of the comforts of home."

"That must have been awful. I can't imagine what you went through!" Aidryan cooed and patted his shoulder.

"It wasn't a favorite time in my life, but little did I know, things were going to get a whole lot worse. One fateful day, my parents decided to leave me at the camp to look for a specific albino tiger that inhabited the area. I happily waved goodbye because I was used to being alone for short periods of time while they did their stuff. Well, a few hours passed, and I started to get a bit worried. I went out to look for them just as a nasty storm started brewing."

"Oh, we know how awful some storms can be. They can be so bad that you could run into a tree if you aren't careful," Dagon added.

Aidryan got his joke and leaned toward him. "If Maylis were here right now, you would be in big trouble."

Chase, not being in on the joke, continued his story. "Yeah, so the storm was coming on very rapidly, and I was too focused on finding my parents at that point to take any precautions. Finally, it hit. I could barely see a foot in front of me. Even my super heavy coat wasn't protecting me from the blistering wind. I'd say I was wandering around for a solid hour. Man, was I terrified! I gave up searching for my parents, thinking that they had probably made it back to camp already. I imagined them waiting for me with warm food and pleasant hugs. I thought I was going the correct way home until I noticed a tree that I had marked before, which told me I had been going in circles. Naturally, I was lost."

Chase took a deep breath and stopped talking. Both Aidryan and Dagon could tell this was a very emotional subject for him and let him take his time to continue the story. Dagon felt that if he were in the same situation, he would have given up a long time ago. Chase paused for a little while longer as if he didn't know how to explain the rest of the story.

"At any rate, I ended up taking shelter in the place you see now, although it was much different then, obviously. I figured it was the best thing to do in that circumstance. So I just curled up and slept. I was never able to find my way back to camp. So for about ten years now, I've been living in this place and going out every single day to search for my mom and dad. It's been a pretty difficult life so far, but I've dealt with everything that's come my way and learned to survive. I have to believe that I was meant to live here. I hold on to the hope that I will one day see my parents again."

Aidryan and Dagon sat still and attempted to comprehend all the heart-wrenching information that this boy had given them. Dagon was the first to break the silence. "I'm truly sorry this happened to you, but I also congratulate you for making it this far and having such a great attitude about it."

"Yeah," Aidryan added, "you are so brave to have done all that at only seven years old! If there is anything we can do to help you out in any way, we would be glad to do it."

"Thanks for your sympathy, but I'm doing just fine on my own. I'm used to living in a world where there are no people or technology or school, as a matter a fact. I get my education from living off the land. But you can help me by staying for a night before you go on your way. I haven't seen a boy or girl my age in so many years. It would be nice to learn a little something about the outside world," Chase suggested.

Dagon and Aidryan exchanged looks and turned back to Chase, telling him it would be their honor to stay the night. He was overjoyed to make two new friends, especially since he didn't have any besides the occasional snowman he built. Chase quickly got up and showed them to two tiny guest rooms. Both Aidryan and Dagon could tell they would be the first ones to use them.

"Oh, so I remember you said you were here on a quest. Can you tell me more about it?" asked Chase.

Dagon turned to his cousin, and she excused them to have a private talk. Chase went outside.

"Should we tell him?" Dagon whispered.

"Of course we should, Dag! Who else is he going to tell, the snowmen?" Aidryan bellowed. "Plus, he knows this place well so he could show us around. We would have a much easier time trying to find the third coin with a guide."

"You're right, but does this have anything to do with the fact that you find him attractive?"

Aidryan swiftly covered his mouth to shush him and looked around for Chase. "It would be best if we didn't talk about that out loud. I don't want to have that conversation with you ever again in my life. Oh, and if you ever *do* bring it up again, I will give you a matching bruise on the other side of your head. I don't care if a troll gets in my way because it will be done." She pulled her hand from his mouth and headed toward the kitchen to see what Chase had to eat in his pantry.

After ten minutes of giving Aidryan some space, Dagon heard Chase come back inside. A wild animal of some kind was draped over his shoulder, dead and wilting.

"Dinner will be ready in a bit. I just have to prepare this guy," Chase said.

Aidryan motioned to Dagon that now was the time to explain their arrival. "So you asked about our quest. Well, we are actually searching for a platinum coin with a letter on it, believe it or not. We need five of them to get into the place where we live."

"Why do you need coins to get into your own house?"

"Well, it's sort of a castle, and we've never been there before."

"Well, that would explain it."

"We can tell you more later. I'm pretty hungry, and that thing you're cooking smells amazing," Aidryan cut in.

For the remainder of the night, Chase and his new friends talked, laughed, and told stories about their childhood.

"Good night, you guys. Thanks for staying with me for a little bit, it means a lot," Chase said.

"It was really nice meeting you too," Aidryan answered.

There was silence for a moment, then Chase came up with an idea. "I think I'd like to take you around tomorrow and show you what I do every day. What do you think?"

"That would be great," Dagon and Aidryan said in unison.

THE BLINDING OWL

Dagon and Aidryan slept better than they ever had on their journey. Chase was busy preparing leftovers in the kitchen. The happy expression on his face showed how nice it was for him to have human company after nearly ten whole years. Aidryan remarked to Dagon how refined Chase was even after not being around other humans for such a long time. Dagon, of course, rolled his eyes because he knew Chase used his exploding dynamite again to kill last night's dinner, but he figured he'd preserve Chase's perfect image for her. They shared a wonderful conversation around the breakfast table about all of the modern luxuries that Chase had never heard of. Smart phones and Bluetooth were some of his favorites. He indicated that when and if he ever came back to civilization, his new friends would have to help him "get connected."

After breakfast Chase made sure that everyone had a warm fur coat on top of their normal clothes, sealed snow boots, scarves, tough gloves, and hats that covered their ears. A few bags were packed full of essential supplies and the safety rules of the area were discussed in exquisite detail. Finally, they were off. The foreign visitors were having the time of their lives rolling around in the snow, taking in the breathtaking views, and starting snowball fights.

Dagon glanced over at Aidryan from time to time. Each time he did so, it felt like she was becoming more and more a part of this strange new world. This scared him a bit because of what happened with Maylis and Zennith just a short time ago. He certainly didn't want to complete this quest all by himself. Then again, Dagon would argue that he'd never seen Aidryan so happy. That radiant smile never left her face, and Chase was always right there ready to share a hearty laugh. Aidryan never had a boyfriend, although, naturally, many boys at school admired her from afar. If they would pluck up the courage to ask her out, she would simply say she wasn't interested. Dagon had seen many of the rejects rushing to the bathroom and slamming the stall door. If he asked what was wrong, they would sniffle and say they didn't want to talk about it. Aidryan was never mean, but she was always an independent girl. Dagon saw that same independence and freedom in her right now in the snow with Chase by her side.

The three of them continued on their snowy walk. Chase mentioned a few facts about what they were seeing. Aidryan was listening attentively, of course, while Dagon searched for a shimmer of platinum. They were here for a reason. No matter how much Aidryan wanted to ignore it, there was a job to do. As if the universe had gone inside his brain and saw his thoughts, a familiar shimmer now caught his eye. Dagon looked at the spot and got a painful beam of light in his eyes for his trouble. He swore it was the coin, but his brief blindness said otherwise.

"*Whoa!* That must be the Blinding Owl you told me about," Aidryan declared.

Chase gazed upward, smiling. "That's right! They're a bit smaller and have larger beaks than snowy owls. Wait hold on. What's that in his mouth?"

Dagon hurried over. "Aidryan look, it's a platinum coin! I bet it has an *I* on the back of it!" Dagon expected Aidryan to be excited.

Instead, disappointment was plastered on her face. She tried to hide it. "*Wow*, that's wonderful news!"

Dagon looked away from the dangerous owl and used his magic to summon the coin. The owl resisted. Eventually, they procured the coin, returned to Chase's home, and began packing to leave. Dagon was nearly finished when Aidryan slid into his room to talk. He instantly knew something was wrong, so he led her to a rickety chair and sat her down.

"What's wrong Aidryan? We're leaving soon. We're *so* close to finally reaching Lamin. All of our training is finally paying off," he said.

"I know, and I'm excited about that . . . but something's changed." She took a deep breath, ready to say her next sentence. "I want to stay here with Chase a little longer."

Dagon couldn't speak for a moment. "So you're going to leave me too, just like Maylis and Zennith? I had a hunch that you liked Chase a little *too* much, but I didn't think you would actually stay with him and leave me to go by myself!"

Aidryan's face fell, knowing he was very right. She told Dagon how she didn't want to leave him but Chase was also alone. She thought he could learn so many new things about the modern world from her and maybe even come to Lamin with her in time.

Dagon felt hurt and pretty stressed at this point. His faith in the quest faltered. He didn't like his odds of winning this argument. He saw with his own eyes how happy Aidryan and Chase were when they were together and how Aidryan's whole face lit up whenever their eyes met. No matter how hard he tried, he just couldn't let that go. He sat in his chair with his hands held tightly together and took a deep breath. He smiled at Aidryan, her face hopeful. "I think it would be fine for you to stay with him a little longer," he said.

Chase heard the entire conversation from the living room, which didn't surprise Dagon in the slightest. He bolted in as soon as Dagon finished. He said a hearty thank you and hugged him tightly as well. They stayed in the room a little longer to help Dagon get all his belongings together. Aidryan carefully wrapped the newest addition to their coin collection and added it to the pouch. She double-checked to make sure all four of them were there. Dagon whistled for Rarity who was off trying to find grass for a snack. From the irritated look on her face, he guessed she wasn't successful. Chase helped Aidryan harness her up while Dagon did one more sweep of the house. Then Chase helped him load his stuff into the carriage. It was time for goodbyes.

"Good-bye, Chase. I really appreciate you saving me and Aidryan when we first got here. We'd have been dead if it weren't for you and your dynamite," Dagon said, giving him another hug. When he turned to Aidryan, she raised her eyebrow at the mention of dynamite, but being the smart girl she was, she decided to let it go. When Dagon took another look at his stuff, he saw that Aidryan slipped him a note along with her hair clip sword. The note read, "Use it. Don't lose it." He stuck his head out the nearest window to wave, and they *whooshed* out of the mountains toward the blue sky.

Dagon took a few minutes to straighten up the carriage because Rarity's takeoff had been bumpier than usual. He yawned and found a comfortable spot to rest his head for the next leg of his journey. Just before drifting off, his mind went to Zennith and Aidryan's families as well as his own mother. It must have taken a lot of courage for them to let their kids attempt this quest, not knowing if or when they would see them again. Dagon thought about his mom and the many happy times they spent together just the two of them. Dagon pictured his mom and himself as a kid having a delicious picnic after they went on one of their many hikes through the woods. He saw her smile perfectly in his brain, which made him smile in his sleep.

A few hours later, a deafening noise awakened him. Rarity called to him from up front and explained that she was experiencing strong turbulence. Dagon clambered to the front so he could see Rarity properly through the tiny windows.

"Just hold on," he said. "We can make it through this, I know we can!"

35

SNOW-COVERED PAST

"And that is how you make a snow shovel," Chase said while Aidryan examined it. "It's great for digging yourself out of drifts or scaring away trolls that want to eat the food you packed, no matter how scarce a portion it is."

Aidryan giggled and handed the finished product back to Chase. They sat on the ground surrounded by snow and various weapons and inventions that had been useful to Chase over the years. He was taking this time so his friend would get used to living in the wild gradually, instead of being forced into it as he was. Dagon had been gone for a few hours. As much as she missed him, Aidryan was content with her decision.

Chase's next lesson for her was to learn how to hunt. Apparently, swatting shovels at prey doesn't count. Aidryan was skeptical at first but was always up for trying something new, especially if she could be good at it. Chase grabbed a bow and some arrows, took her hand, and led her to a practice target that, from the looks of it, had been used and abused by many arrows and even an occasional spear. "I've set up many of these targets over time to improve my aim. As I got better, my targets got father away and more challenging. This is the first one I made. You're going to start here as well."

"Okay, so if I hit the target with an arrow, I can advance?" she inquired.

Chase smirked. "Not exactly," he said. He handed her the bow and dropped a quiver of arrows on the ground beside her. "You have to hit a bull's-eye at least ten times in a row to continue."

Aidryan's jaw dropped. "What? That could take days, if not weeks!"

"Well, if it's too challenging for you, then you can stay home and cook while I go out and hunt." Although they had only been at this for one day, it seemed like Chase had already found Aidryan's weakness of having to prove she could do anything a guy could. Chase left to go back inside, assuming that he had a while to wait before she hit all ten arrows in the very center. Once he was completely out of view, Aidryan got to work. Some time later, Aidryan knocked on Chase's door. She dropped the empty quiver on the doorstep in front of him. Anxious to see how she did, he grabbed his boots and coat and trailed after her. Sure enough, all ten arrows were stuck in the center of the target. "If you think you can get away with using magic to fake these shots, then you've got another thing coming," Chase joked.

"How would you even find out in the first place? Would a gossipy owl tell you?" she joked back. "Actually, the owl wouldn't tell you anything because what you see here is all skill."

"Okay, Robin Hood, I believe you for now. But you know those owls just love to talk."

Aidryan's training went faster than expected so they were out hunting in just a few short days. They even had a schedule already. They would get up when the sun did, prepare some breakfast, and head out the door with their weapons, ready to find what they'd be bringing home that day for dinner. Today was going especially well. They trailed off to their usual hunting sites and spotted a deer feeding on a patch of grass. Aidryan made her mark, pulled back her hand until it touched the tip of her cheek, then let the arrow fly. Chase gave her a nice clap when it hit its target, and she bowed dramatically. On their way back, Aidryan suggested they try a new place to hunt.

"It would be exciting," she said.

Chase rolled his eyes. He was hunched over because he had a good-sized buck draped across his shoulders. The boy agreed but insisted they drop their catch off at home. Aidryan traipsed through the snowy woods, not particularly thinking about any-thing. Chase followed suit, carrying no large animals this time. Twenty minutes in, the kids came across a small bluff with a breathtaking view.

"What do you think, Robin Hood?" he asked, taking her hand.

"It's beautiful!" Aidryan walked along the ridge, looking for another vantage point. She went pretty far before calling to Chase. "Come see this!"

"Okay, hold on, I'm coming!" He jogged toward Aidryan's voice but stopped short when he heard a yelp coming from the same direction. Chase immediately assumed the worst and ran faster to the spot. As soon as he arrived, he sighed with relief. Aidryan had fallen on a soft spot between the tree roots and was standing up to her chest in dirt. He laughed and pulled her out of the hole. Aidryan shook the dirt and snow off her clothes while Chase examined the opening. Then he remembered something. "Wait a minute! I think this is one of my dad's old hunting traps! There used to be a tunnel . . " He jumped back into the hole. Sure enough, he found the narrow passageway. He called up to Aidryan to come check it out so she jumped in. They began to crawl. A few minutes later, they reached the end of the underground shaft and found themselves in a small cave. A faint light glowed from a crack in the opposite wall. "Aidryan, do you realize where we are? This is the camp that I lived in with my parents!" Textbooks about science, old pictures, maps, a rickety wooden desk, and even some childish drawings Chase had made so long ago dotted the room. He took a look around, his head filling with memories of his life with his parents. He was used to it now but learning to survive alone in the harsh mountain climate had been a harrowing experience.

Aidryan saw the look on his face and got an idea. She turned to Chase and spoke so loudly that he almost dropped the bunny drawing he was holding. "Hey! What if we fix this place up? That way, we could stay here to hunt or use it if something goes wrong at your other place. Not that it would, of course, but still."

After Chase contemplated the idea, he agreed to help Aidryan with her new project. He almost declined but then remembered she was nearly as good a sharpshooter as he was and didn't want her to poke him with arrows, so he smiled and gave his blessing. The next few days were solely dedicated to perfecting the second camp. Occasionally, Aidryan would forget they had to eat so Chase would excuse himself to go hunting.

By the end of the week, Aidryan considered the project accomplished. She took a step back to admire all of the work they'd put in to making this a livable space again. There were now larger windows, a new wooden door (courtesy of Chase's ax skills), two warm beds with extra blankets (sheets picked out by Aidryan and bedframes made by Chase), tables and chairs, and even a rudimentary kitchen. Aidryan was proud of her work and was especially pleased that Chase had been willing to help. Fixing things made her feel like she was in complete control of her life, and she needed that. Nevertheless, fixing up a house like this made her miss the one she had back home and all her friends and family along with it.

"Are you okay?" Chase asked.

They were sitting at the table in the new house. Aidryan held a cup of water in her hand but paid no attention to it. She was gazing out the window, lost in thought. Chase tried again.

"Earth to Aidryan, what's wrong? I'm getting pretty nervous over here."

"It's nothing, really. I just miss my friends and my family and my home. I'll get over it soon, I promise."

"Aidryan—" Chase began, but Aidryan cut him off abruptly as if she didn't want anyone to know she was hurting.

"Don't worry about me. I'll be back to my old self soon enough. Come on, let's go hunting." She got up, grabbed her stuff by the door, and began putting on her boots.

Chase got up and stopped her. "No, wait! I think you should think about this a little more. I don't want to keep you from your old life, and I especially don't want you to be unhappy, even if that means that you're not with me."

After hearing his statement, Aidryan flung a boot across the room, hitting some stacked books that fell with a crash. She reached out to Chase. He embraced her as she collapsed into a ball of tears.

"It's okay. I'm sorry I upset you. That was never my intention," Chase said softly while lightly stroking her long hair.

"It's not you. I'm sorry I freaked out on you," she said through sniffles.

"Whatever you want to do, I'll support you."

"That's the problem, I have no idea what I want to do."

36

THE CAVE

The constant jolting of the carriage was not a good way for Dagon to wake up. He would have preferred a nice, warm cup of soothing coffee rather than climbing aboard this roller coaster.

"Rarity!" he called to the front. "We need to get out of the sky. Land somewhere *safe*—and fast!"

She turned to him, looking worried (as far as Dagon could tell since pegasi don't have eyebrows). Dagon clambered to the back of the carriage to think and strategize.

BOOM! A bolt of lightning surged through the carriage, causing Dagon to stumble and land on his arm in the process. He called out in pain, then was hit by a loose decoration. He saw blackness as every thought left his mind.

Dagon woke up groggy with his left arm throbbing. He figured this was how Aidryan must have felt after being knocked out by the troll. He glanced around for Rarity but heard no noise. He slowly stood up to get a better vantage point to search for his friend. Dagon was standing on a beach on what appeared to be another island, looking out onto a very rowdy ocean. It was cold and dismal. The color of the sky reflected the weather. For the first time in a long time, he was completely alone with only the sounds of nature filling the deafening silence. He had a choice, search for Rarity and hope the universe gave him a free pass to keep at least one friend on this voyage or simply do nothing and wait for a miracle. Instead of addressing the question, he contemplated how he would fix his swelling arm. (Procrastination, even magical beings have trouble with it sometimes.) Since focusing would be too challenging at this point, he did a quick spell that put his arm in a sling. Now he could go on his search for Rarity.

He whipped around to face the opposite direction and nearly jumped back. This particular island happened to be one part thick trees and one part humongous boulders, both of which shielded his view quite entirely. He chuckled. *If this had been easy, I would have known something was off,* he joked quietly to himself. Dagon began walking toward the center of the island with no clue as to what his next move should be. Wandering into a dense forest without any supplies or sense of direction is exactly what crazy people would do. That thought was circling in Dagon's head constantly as he scrambled over jagged rocks and fallen trees. He figured this way would be easier than attempting to climb the towering boulders. Having very little magic powers at the moment, this seemed like the better option.

Traveling without his winged companion was weighing on him. He was getting increasingly annoyed at the fact that his brain was working more slowly than usual, and he had yet to think of a sane solution. Dagon kept thinking how tall and wide those mountains were and how even the smaller ones weren't small. If only he could get to the top of one of those smaller ones, he could see more clearly. Maybe all his problems would be solved. That spark of hope soothed his confidence. With a huge breath, he began his ascent of the nearest smallest mountain. Getting to the top was not as difficult as Dagon imagined. Sure, there were obstacles and sometimes he felt like he was going to fall backward because of the incredible steepness, but his determination outweighed all that. He took a deep breath and yelled out for his friend. He tried that a couple of times but soon just ended up shouting for her to find some food for him.

"Hey, let's go, Rarity! I need some of those fruity gummies we packed" and "I am about to die on this gigantic hill right now, and I'm so blaming it on *you*!" Next, it was, "Okay, listen, I'm sorry about what I said before. I'm just really hungry, and my stomach is getting the better of me. *I'm* not yelling at you, my stomach is!" And finally, "Just please come and find me. I've been involuntarily hiking for hours. I really want to see you again so please find me. Don't leave without me." After his mini rant to no one in particular, he sat down on the prickly grass and prepared himself for whatever the future might hold. Dagon closed his eyes and concentrated on calming himself down so he could think more clearly.

"Done screaming so soon?" joked a voice from behind him.

He whipped around and saw Rarity. "Wha—what the heck! I called for you like fifty times! *Now* you decide to show yourself?"

"*Whoa*, calm down, mountain boy! I've only been here for a few minutes. I did think it was cute how you said you didn't want me to leave without you. It really made me smile." She flashed her horsey teeth.

"You . . . you..." Dagon sputtered, but he was too hungry and irritated to pursue it.

As Dagon ate his gummies, Rarity told him how she felt fine when they landed and decided to fly around and explore a little. She explained that she found a cave relatively close by and wanted to go inside, but she still had the carriage attached to her so that just wasn't an option. Dagon helped her out of her harness and pushed the carriage behind a boulder. The food gave him enough strength to concentrate on his arm. After it was healed, he hopped on Rarity's back, and she flew them to the cave.

"At least this one's not underwater," he joked.

Rarity didn't get the joke since she was not in existence when that situation occurred. Once they reached the entrance, Dagon climbed down from Rarity's back and wasted no time searching for symbols and clues. He turned to her. "There doesn't seem to be any dead giveaways on why this cave is here. It looks like I'll have to go inside." She agreed and told him she would stay outside to keep watch since her wings could not easily fit into the space. So Dagon was pretty much on his own, again.

He had ventured into so many unknown places on this journey but was still nervous every time. This place was no exception, especially now that he didn't have three friends with him for backup and moral support. Acknowledging this did nothing to ease his anxiety. Before him was a narrow hallway that led into blackness. Unfortunately, Dagon had left his trusty headlamp in the carriage. He inched his way step by step, feeling the sidewalls at the same time to avoid bumping into something that could give him nightmares. That process seemed to be working until he smashed his face against a wall in front of him. That was painful but also worked to his advantage because as he collided with it, his shoulder must have hit something that made the wall turn and flip him over to the other side. It was a convenient but alarming experience. He peeled his face off the musty wall and turned around. He stood on a steep precipice overlooking a mountain of buildings and artifacts that filled the entire space. There was a window built into the top of the cave that let in enough light to make everything shimmer. Then Dagon saw the familiar Laminian symbol painted on the wall straight ahead as if it knew he would come.

Dagon analyzed his approach. Getting to the floor would not be easy. He got down on his stomach and slowly scooted toward the edge of the platform until his head, neck, and half of his body were in danger of falling over and taking the rest of him with it. His ability to formulate idiot-proof plans was wearing thin. He inched himself back from the devastating drop-off and steadied himself by grabbing a coarse rope hanging nearby. He glanced to his left and soon a smile began to form. "I got this," he said aloud, hoping that if any strange cave dwellers were watching him, they would know how awesome he was.

He pulled the rope in the direction of the steep drop-off and used his weight to test if it would hold him if he swung through the air like a magical Tarzan. It *seemed* sturdy. At this point, he was willing to risk it. The rope was attached to a small alcove in the ceiling. If he aimed right, he could drop down on the flat roof of the main building. From there, he could easily slide off to the safety of the floor. *This is a good plan*, he thought. *However, if Rarity were here, she would definitely not think so.* Actually, if Rarity and her wings were just a tiny bit smaller, then this Tarzan leap would be completely unnecessary. But focusing on the negative was not going to help him in any way, shape, or form; so he redirected his focus to the task at hand.

Dagon took a deep breath and got into position. He grabbed the rope, shouted, "I can do this!" with gusto and *whooshed* through the air. The beginning of the ride was not as scary as he thought, but as he got close to the landing strip, his opinion changed. "Oh no!" he yelled as he began to kick his legs in a meaningless attempt to slow down. Then it was time for him to let go. "One . . . two . . . three!" He let go. With a hard *thump*, he found himself lying face down on the metal roof. "Wonderful," he moaned.

In too much pain to get up, Dagon stayed perfectly still rethinking his whole plan and picking out everything that was wrong with it. There were a lot of examples. His sedentary state was also due to the fact that any potential cave dwellers were probably laughing at him right now, and he wanted to avoid their mockery. After enjoying this short respite, he figured he shouldn't lie around all day, leaving Rarity to worry about him. He pulled himself to his feet and carefully climbed down a rickety pillar to the floor. At the bottom, he found a tiny pedestal with words engraved on it. He read the message aloud. "If treasure is what you seek, then you're looking on the wrong level." That made absolutely no sense to him. He repeated the clue over and over in his head to try and solve it. He looked on the floor for a magic button he could press and pushed on the pedestal to see if it opened a hidden doorway. Nothing worked. He slumped down to the floor and groaned. He tried to get up again but hit the top of his head on the bottom of the pedestal. Something clicked.

He slinked out from underneath the pedestal and got up. The engraved message had disappeared. A shiny coin had taken its place. He leaned over, grabbed it, and checked the back. Sure enough, there was a Laminian *N* etched on the back with the familiar Laminian symbol on the front. He had found the last coin. Dagon wasted no more time in that death-defying cave. He scurried back up the rope and ran to where Rarity was waiting for him. He showed her the coin and vowed he would never willingly go back in another cave as long as he lived. Rarity whinnied in agreement. Dagon stashed the coin in the pouch with the others and magically glued the bag to the floor of the carriage for safe-keeping. Dagon and Rarity spent the rest of the day talking fondly about their time spent with Zennith, Aidryan, and Maylis. Rarity told Dagon what it felt like to be turned into a flying horse after being a simple pool chair. Dagon told the story of how the four kids met and came to be on this quest in the first place. They decided to stay on the island for a few more days so Dagon could regain his strength.

A few days turned into a few weeks. Time seemed to fade from existence on this island. Soon, all Dagon cared about was having time to think about everything and nothing in particular. He woke up every morning and took a long walk on the beach, then he'd lie down and let the pounding waves crash over him. Occasionally, he would charm himself so he could breathe underwater. Then he would just glide along for hours, following the fish as if he were one of them. It got to the point where Rarity spent most of her days worrying about him and searching the water for signs that he was still alive. When she felt anxious, she took to the sky where she could spread her wings and feel free. The question of when they would continue the quest had come up in past conversations, but Dagon waved it off every time. He kept saying there was no point now that his friends had all moved on and found new destinies. Dagon argued that this island was his new destiny. Rarity usually let Dagon vent, but she decided to confront him about her concerns. She had come too far to crash-land on an uninhabited island and not finish what she was made to do. So she decided to confront him about her concerns. That morning when she heard him rustling inside the carriage, she spoke her mind and didn't waste any time about it.

"Okay, listen, Dagon, we have come too far to give up now. I'm not going to stay here and watch you throw the quest away to swim with fish."

Dagon had barely stepped foot out of the carriage before being confronted and needed a few seconds to process what had just been said to him. He did, however, grumble after her insulting comment concerning the fish he'd grown fond of. There was a long pause. "I understand what you're saying, Rarity, but I don't see the harm in staying a little while longer."

Now it was Rarity's turn to groan. "I didn't want to say this, but don't you think your mom would want you to return to the place you were born and complete your quest?"

Dagon didn't say anything.

"Doesn't she deserve to see you at least try to finish what you started? I know that she would be so pleased to know you went home to help your father defeat that evil scoundrel Erex and take your rightful place as the prince of Lamin. Don't you want to meet your dad anymore?"

Dagon sighed and took another step out of the carriage to look Rarity straight in the eyes. She met his gaze, anticipating his answer. "Let's go meet my dad."

WRONG MOVE

No time was wasted in preparing for their long overdue departure from that alluring piece of land. Dagon regained his eagerness to return to his mysterious birthplace, and Rarity's mood improved every moment they spent getting ready. Soon it came time to fly. Rarity was all suited up in her harness. Dagon was in the carriage, taking care of last-minute details when fate fluctuated and sent their goals spiraling backward into oblivion. The carriage began to shake tremendously and set Dagon off balance, making him have sudden flashbacks of how they arrived on this island in the first place.

"Rarity, what's wrong?"

"*Uh*, I'm not quite sure," she answered. "Something's happening to me!"

"I'm coming!" he yelled. Toppling out of the unsteady carriage, he ran straight to his friend. "Rarity, you're shrinking!" he gasped.

"Stay back! I don't want you to get hurt!"

Reluctantly, Dagon inched backward. Rarity's body kept deflating and her form glowed. Dagon stood there, feeling completely helpless and scared. Then a sudden blast of energy sent him flying into a tree. He was knocked out cold. Dagon came to just before dark. His thoughts were fuzzy, and his head hurt from the impact. Then the memory of Rarity's struggle came flooding back in an enormous dark cloud. Guilt and failure spread through him like wildfire, and he gave in to it. He was afraid to go over and see the wreckage but knew that was exactly what he had to do. The carriage had toppled over. Tree branches were pushed through its windows. He looked frantically for the coin pouch and found it still glued to the carriage floor intact. Finally, he approached the last place he saw Rarity before the explosion. What he saw brought tears to his eyes. A beach chair—a chaise lounge, to be exact—was lying disheveled on the ground.

This set Dagon off. He exploded into a fit of rage, throwing various objects as he cried harder than he ever had before. He stood there shaking with bolts of magical energy flying from his body. So many friends had left him. Even though he knew they never meant to hurt him, his heart ached from their abandonment. Now Dagon had not only lost his equine friend, but also his ticket off the island. How would he ever get to Lamin now?

I got it! He thought. Dagon jogged down to the lagoon where his aquatic acquaintances liked to hang out. Sure enough, his buddy Larry was chilling out in a bit of seaweed.

"Hey, Larry! How's it going?" Dagon called.

"Yo, Dagon. Wassup?"

"So, Lar, something's come up. I need to get to the main city of Lamin as soon as possible. Do you know anyone who might be able to get me there?" Dagon asked.

"*Hmmm.* Let me think about that one." Larry tapped his gills with his fins. "My cousin Sheila runs a taxi business, but I'm pretty sure it's restricted to water destinations. You know, Mr. Jelly might be able to fly you there. Why don't you ask him?"

Dagon frowned. "A flying jellyfish?"

"Whoever heard of a flying jellyfish?" Larry exclaimed. "Mr. Jelly is a pelican who runs a catering business out of Lamin. He comes to the island all the time for supplies. In fact, he's picking up an order at Creative Caviar for a big wedding tomorrow night. You should be able to catch him if you leave now."

Fast-forward to the end of a very long night when Dagon and Mr. Jelly finally arrived at the outskirts of Lamin. Far off in the distance, Dagon could just make out the pointy turrets of a castle—*his* castle. He was just about to politely ask Mr. Jelly to hang a right when something caught his eye. A figure in a jet-black ninja suit and full coverage facemask was cornering a terrified family. Dagon asked the pelican to drop him off in a secluded spot behind some bushes. "Thanks for the ride, Mr. Jelly. I'll be all right from here." Dagon said.

"Anytime, son. Enjoy your stay in Lamin." Mr. Jelly flew off as Dagon turned to face the creepy thug. "Hey!" he called out in his lowest voice.

The figure whipped around to see Dagon suspended a few feet in the air with his hands on his hips (Dagon thought he would strike more fear if he entered looking like a superhero). Unfortunately, his rival had magical powers as well. He twisted his hand slightly and sent a gust of wind, knocking Dagon to the ground. The family scurried away. His opponent didn't speak a word but from the way his hands began spitting fire, Dagon figured this ninja man was ready for a fight. Dagon attacked first, using a water sword he created from a nearby stream to extinguish the flames, but the enemy outmaneuvered him and threw a fireball at Dagon's leg. The burn made him cry out but he wouldn't back down. Dagon turned his sword into a bow and fired one arrow after another, but the dark ninja avoided every one. He threw a boulder at Dagon's face. Dagon dive-rolled behind a tree to catch his breath. Whoever or whatever this guy was, he had obviously been trained by someone a bit more experienced and agile than Maylis (meaning no offence to his friend, of course).

Dagon leaned his head against the back of the tree, sighed deeply, and reappeared from behind it, wielding another water sword and shield. He took his stance in front of the villain and waited. Dagon was going to play defense this time. Once more, they collided. This time the ninja created a water sword as well. He struck first, making Dagon struggle to block his opponent's flashing sword. This went on for quite a while, and Dagon began to lose steam. But then he had an idea, a last resort in beating this guy. He dropped his sword and used that hand to control the water in the stream. He sent a huge wave toppling over his opponent. The ninja wizard tumbled and tumbled underneath the sudden tsunami until Dagon couldn't see him anymore. He kept his hands focused on the water for a few more seconds just in case. The villain was now twenty feet away and not moving. Dagon walked in that direction to survey the damage he had done but soon realized he should have done more. His opponent began sputtering and spitting out water. He was still alive and was undoubtedly annoyed. Dagon didn't need evidence to draw that conclusion. Then the ninja spoke.

"Well done, Dagon, prince of Lamin. I have to admit, I didn't know what to expect from you at our first meeting. I'm so glad I caught you before you reached your father's house."

"I would like to know with *whom* I am fighting," Dagon snapped, using his best grammar for effect.

"Oh, I think you've heard of me. I'm the reason you came back, am I not? My name is Erex. You might know me as Lamin's worst nightmare."

38

AN OLD REMINDER

There are many different levels of stalking. They can range from just keeping an eye on someone to a full-on have-no-life psycho obsession. However, there are some rare exceptions to this rule. One of these rare exceptions happened to be someone the friends knew and loved, the cave-dwelling shape-shifter, Sarina. They may have loved her a tad less if they knew she'd been watching their every move, but in her defense, she was only doing it because she cared about them. That and the fact her life was not very eventful at the moment.

Since her departure from the cave, she'd visited many places that were not underwater and observed many humans and their twenty-first century ways. She found it very educational. But from time to time on her travels, she would stop and check in on the kids who made it possible for her to finally satisfy her wanderlust. She witnessed the exciting water balloon fight, the kids' adventures on Gobique Island, and their fight with Gnith. She watched Aidryan make a new friend and knew Dagon was now on his own to finish the quest. She hated to interfere but watching Dagon battle Erex made it necessary—and urgent.

The ex-guardian was currently staying in a cheap hotel in New York City. It was there she decided to use a portal message to reach the kids. She centered herself on the bed and waved her hands to expose three mini swirling pools on the wall in front of her. It only took a few seconds for the faces of Aidryan, Zennith, and Maylis to form within the circles.

"Hello, my dears. Miss me?" Sarina asked with a hearty laugh.

"Hey, Sarina!" Zennith shouted.

"Sarina!" exclaimed Aidryan. "It's so nice to see you . . . well, sort of see you. If you count looking through a portal as seeing you, then it really is nice!"

With his usual aplomb, Maylis got right to the point. "Hi, Sarina! What's wrong?"

"Now I don't blame you for anything you are about to hear, my dears," Sarina answered, "but your friend Dagon is in a tricky situation. He ran into Erex at the Laminian border and was bashed up quite a bit. Dagon is in need of some assistance."

"Hold on! Aidryan, you left him too?" asked Zennith.

"*Ugh!* Can we talk about this later?" Aidryan groaned.

"Let's just focus on the more important task at hand," Sarina intervened. "So will you go or not?"

"There's no question about what we are going to do," Aidryan loudly declared. "We have to help him."

"Absolutely!" Maylis agreed.

"Can we just take a second to discuss why the two of you left the quest? I may have started a revolution, but I certainly didn't expect anyone to join it," Zennith said.

"It isn't that simple. We just did what we felt was right at the time. We may have gotten the idea from you, but these were our decisions!" Aidryan snapped, feeling a bit attacked.

"I found my uncle Maurice in Egypt, and I couldn't just pick up and leave before we got reacquainted," explained Maylis.

"Oh, yeah. By the way, how was Egypt? See any creepy mummies or cursed treasure?" Zennith asked, getting off track.

"We are supposed to be focusing on Dagon right now!" Aidryan interjected.

"Fine. We'll catch up when we all meet *after* we help Dagon out of the Erex-sized pickle he's gotten himself into," he compromised. "Now let's finish this conversation because the little princess is getting salty."

"I—" Aidryan started.

"All right, all right! Enough!" Sarina yelled. "This is taking far too much time, and I don't want to sit here and listen to a bunch of teenagers arguing. If I wanted to hear that, I would turn on *Teen Wolf*. Now, my dears, I'm going to ask you one last time. Are you ready to go to Lamin to rescue your best friend?"

"Well, technically, you can only really have one best—"

"That's enough, Zennith! Trust me, I can find a way to portal slap you one way or another, you can bet on that," Sarina threatened, smiling as she did so.

"Just ignore him. Of course I'll go!" Aidryan said.

"Count me in," Maylis added.

"Out of the safety of our new lives and into a battle with Erex," Zennith sighed. "What are we waiting for?"

39

Good Riddance

Dagon already had a rough couple of days, and the fact that he was currently being tied to a tree with scratchy ropes and more pressure than a hungry boa constrictor clearly demonstrated that his stress pile was adding up. Erex soon finished, but just before he tied the last knot, he added an extra tug that constricted the air in Dagon's lungs, just to prove he'd won. He gave Dagon a harsh look from behind his mask and took a supplementary pause before turning his back and slowly walking off to a nearby rock to sit down. This was when Dagon's heart stopped. The villainous ninja removed his black mask, revealing his face. Erex looked just like Dagon's father. He had seen pictures of his dad throughout the history books that Maylis had shown him. Although most were outdated, Erex's dark-brown hair and striking light eyes were practically identical to his father's. This meant that he, Dagon, was also an Erex look-alike. Dagon suspected that he, Erex, and his father Klayric were all related.

Dagon was studying this man so intently that he forgot to check his surroundings. If he had, he would have been relieved sooner rather than later. Out of nowhere, six flying folks swooped down from the sky and dive-bombed Erex. They were almost on top of him when the wizard looked up and sprang to one side, causing the furious six to land in an awkward pile next to the rock he had just been sitting on. Dagon was trying to get a good view of these fighters and was having a bit of trouble until Erex shifted slightly to the left, revealing them. Zennith, Mr. Gobique, Chase, Maylis, and Sarina now stood boldly with their weapons in hand.

While the rest of the gang attempted to corner Erex, Aidryan rushed over to Dagon and untied his ropes. Before Dagon could completely untangle himself from them, she threw her arms around him. "We're all so sorry, Dag!" she gasped. "I hope this makes up for it."

"I'll be okay, once you stop hugging me and I can breathe again." He laughed. "Let's get this sucker."

Aidryan nodded as they brought out their weapons and joined the rest of the group. Erex looked concerned at first but produced his deathly water sword once again. He let out a battle cry and charged his adversaries as they did the same. Using his vast capability for fire spells, Zennith held his hand up until it turned an angry shade of red. When Erex's back was turned, Zennith placed his sweltering hand on the villain's shoulder ever so gingerly. That gentleness, however, did nothing to stop the searing pain that radiated into Erex's left shoulder. He crumpled to the ground in agony.

"You think you've won?" Erex bellowed. "This war isn't over yet. I promise when I come back—and I will come back—there will be a reckoning so complete, it will destroy all of you and many others!" He spat in front of them.

Zennith was within the firing zone and quickly stepped back with a disgusted expression. Dagon went in for the kill, but Erex was too quick. "Good-bye, my prince. I will see you again!" Then he vanished in a puff of smoke, leaving no residue behind.

"Good riddance!" Zennith said after he was gone. The rest of them gave him a weird look as if to say how stupid that sounded. "What? It seemed appropriate." A slight chuckle was shared among them as Zen crossed his arms and huffed, mildly annoyed.

A few moments later, they realized that not all of them had been properly introduced. The only greeting they had had was when Sarina transported them from their individual locations to meet in the sky above Lamin. The only words that were exchanged before they dive-bombed the villain were, "Hey!" and "I'm confused. Do we attack him now?"

Chase stepped forward and introduced himself. "I'm Chase. I'm a friend of Aidryan's."

"Yeah, sure you are," Zennith mumbled but not quietly enough.

"I heard that, bud!" Aidryan snapped.

"Hello, Chase, my name is Sarina. They met me quite early on in their journey. They don't know this, but I've been watching over them ever since."

"Are we going to pretend that isn't creepy?" Dagon mumbled to Aidryan.

"I agree with our young prince on the matter of general creepiness, but that's beside the point. Hello, ladies, gentlemen, and stalker. My name is Mr. Gobique. I am a teacher of magic and deception."

Sarina rolled her eyes at the stalker comment but decided not to make a scene. She put her arms around Dagon. "I was really worried about you at first, but then I remembered where you come from and your unbelievable strength and courage. I'm very proud of you."

"Thanks, Sarina. Thanks for organizing the rescue effort. Even with my obvious strength (Aidryan rolled her eyes), Erex was still a tough opponent to beat," Dagon responded.

"Anytime!" She winked.

Now it was Zennith's turn. "Yeah, sorry we left you," Zennith said. "We had no idea leaving would cause so much damage."

"We are never leaving you again." Aidryan smiled and touched Dagon's arm.

Zennith turned to Maylis. "Speaking of leaving, where is your uncle Maurice?"

Maylis sighed. "To be honest, he's kind of old. Although he wanted to, I don't think it would have been good for him to fly, let alone battle an unstoppable villain."

"*Ah!*" Zennith nodded. "What about you, Dag? Where's our dear Rarity?"

Dagon stayed quiet for a while. He needed time to formulate his answer. "I . . . I don't really know," he stammered. "All of a sudden, she just transformed back to the deck chair she was before Aidryan turned her into a pegasus." They all gasped and hung their heads. No one talked for a while after that.

"It'll be okay," Aidryan said softly after the quiet time was over. "She was an incredible help to us. We will always remember her hard work and dedication to the quest. For now, let's focus on how we're going to get to that castle."

"Did you really take out all of those guys by yourself?"

"Oh yes, Chase," boasted Mr. Gobique. "They were very angry teens, and it took a lot of effort on my part to subdue them. I dare say, it was absolutely one of the most difficult tasks I've ever done in my entire career."

"Oh, shush it, G!" Sarina interrupted. "You weren't the one who dragged them all into the closet. Remember, I watched every detail unfold!"

"That may be true," retorted Mr. Gobique. "But at least I didn't open portals to Lamin right under our feet with no warning besides 'Ready, set, go!' If you knew me well, you would know I'm terribly afraid of heights!"

"All right," Aidryan said, taking charge. "We need ideas for transportation. Does anyone have anything?"

"I think you all will like this idea," Maylis started. "I was thinking about using magic (obviously) to create a small plane. It will get us where we need to go, and I don't think anyone will have trouble with the height situation with a sturdy floor beneath their feet."

"He does have a compelling argument," Aidryan said to the group.

"There is no time to waste then!" Dagon announced and clapped his hands together as a sign of approval. Inside, he was regretting this decision already.

No one had any better ideas so a plane it was. Each of the wizards, minus Chase, who just stood there with his mouth open, formed a line facing one of the hills. Some confused Laminian townspeople watched as the kids used their wands to form a powerful flying machine. The scene was exceptionally impressive. Once they were finished, they regrouped to decide who the pilot should be. Maylis was unanimously chosen. Sarina, Chase, and Mr. G started trekking up the hill toward the plane. Dagon took Aidryan, Maylis, and Zennith aside and felt around in his bag for the coins that had been through almost as much as they. He lined them all up on the ground so that the platinum letters were all in formation facing upward. That was when the coins glowed. Not an astonishing glow, but just bright enough that the friends caught a glimpse before the light vanished completely. Sarina and the others had already reached the plane, and they called down to them to follow. Dagon collected each coin and secured them in his bag, double-checking to make sure they'd be safe no matter how badly Maylis flew. The travelers all climbed aboard. Maylis and his copilot, Mr. Gobique, headed to the cockpit to prepare for takeoff.

As they walked toward the plane, Aidryan pulled Dagon aside. "Do you think that Platinums is a good name to call our little group? I've been thinking about what we should call ourselves for a while now."

"You may be on to something, Aidryan. You may be on to something big."

40

Plan of Attack

On the edge of a magnificent mountain, far away from Klayric's castle, civilization and company alike stood a small fortress. Its only entrance was magically sealed so that no amount of strong men or women could unhinge it. There was only a single word that could open the door.

"*Batrachomyomachy!*" Erex articulated.

And just like that, the impenetrable door creaked open. He went inside, clearly in distress. A cement gargoyle perched in a small alcove greeted his master with jubilance.

"Why so down, my master? Was your mission as successful as your music career?"

"*Ugh!* Not now, Milton, I'm sulking." The evil man daintily felt his shoulder but soon regretted it when a dreadful stinging sensation jumped through his entire body.

"Yes, I can see that, my master. But if you don't mind me saying so, sir, someone as evil and manipulative as yourself doesn't need to sulk. Being evilly delighted is more your style."

Erex shot out a hand and wrapped it around Milton's neck. "IF I WANT TO SULK, THEN I WILL SULK!" Erex screamed.

Milton vigorously nodded his stone head as Erex released him and headed toward his study. The sorcerer's sudden outburst didn't keep naive old Milton at bay. He spread his wings, which made a cracking sound almost like rocks falling down a cliff, and flew to his master's side once again. "My master, it just occurred to me that you are not happy with me. Is there anything I can do to make you feel villainous again?" Milton asked, genuinely concerned.

Erex lifted his hand to strike him but stopped and thought for a second. "Why, Milton, it seems as though you are right. Master is very tired from fighting little annoyances all day, so a nice cup of coffee would suit me perfectly."

"Yes, sir! Yes, sir!" Milton said excitedly.

For the next ten minutes, give or take, a quite dense gargoyle named Milton hurried around the mountain lair, searching for coffee ingredients for his evil, very tired master. While his servant bounced off the walls, Erex kicked off his two-inch-high black boots and removed his ninja costume, hanging it up carefully so it would be ready for its next use. The wizard arranged some pillows on his leather La-Z-Boy and eased down into the soft abyss. He pushed a button to raise the footrest, put his bristly hands behind his ears, and shut his eyes. Although it was difficult to rest while his crazed pet swarmed around, banging into various objects and swearing, he knew that cement creatures were not harmed by pointy objects and ignored him for a while.

"Milton!" Erex finally bellowed when he had had enough noise, "When will my coffee be ready? I'm dying of thirst over here!"

Milton, his claws full of coffee grounds and a half empty milk carton, stopped in his tracks and faced him. "Soon, my master! I've gathered all the ingredients. It will not take long to put them together."

"That's what I want to hear!"

Milton nodded again and dove into the kitchen to combine all the ingredients. As this was the first time Milton had prepared coffee, he pondered his next move, shrugged, and dumped everything into a large mug. To break up the coffee grounds, he used an onyx mortar-and-pestle set that had "Mommy's Little Villain"

etched into the bottom. He put the cup in a magical-looking microwave and set the timer. When it dinged, he took it out, gave another shrug, and flew it to his master who was waiting impatiently.

Erex took a small sip. "Milton, if there is one thing you're good at, it's making a cup of coffee for your brilliant master."

Milton puffed up his chest with pride. "Why, I am not deserving of your thanks, my master. How about a nice little show to soothe you?"

"Why not," Erex sighed.

The gargoyle swiveled the La-Z-Boy toward what appeared to be a makeshift stage. He went to a chest stuffed with miscellaneous costumes and picked out a golden bow tie with a matching gold-and-black hat. He darted behind the curtain. "Lights, please," he requested.

Erex sighed again but waved his hand so the audience lights dimmed and the stage became bright and beaming. Music began to play softly in the background but grew louder every second. Before Erex knew what was happening, Milton began heartily singing. Not long after, he belted out a show tune and started kicking while throwing his sparkly hat around. Erex had to keep himself from spitting out his coffee. Milton was halfway through his song when Erex decided his ears had had enough.

"STOP, YOU CRAZY ARCHITECTURAL ORNAMENT! YOU'LL WAKE THE ENTIRETY OF LAMIN AS WELL AS THE KING AND HIS CASTLE!" Erex blurted.

Milton froze mid-kick, threw off his musical gear and hat, and turned down the music. Erex rubbed his sore head as Milton whispered his apologies. "All this chaos is giving me a headache, pet. I still need to figure out what to do about our little prince." Milton concluded his master was in the mood for a heart-to-heart talk, so he grabbed a seat across from him and listened closely. Erex continued, "He's a good fighter, I'll give him that, but he still needs training. I can take advantage of that. Heck! I would've had him if his sniveling little friends hadn't shown up. You have no idea how infuriating it was to be so close to my goal only to become outnumbered and forced to run away like a coward."

"You're no coward, my master—"

"Shut up! I know." Milton went back to his no-talking technique. Erex pressed his fingers together in deep thought. "I need another plan to confront him and his cronies. This time, I will be ready. I know he has some backup, but he doesn't know that I have some friends of my own," he said with a devious smirk.

"Oh my! Does this mean you are going to call *them?*" Milton levitated in suspense.

"It seems I might have to, my winged freak," Erex declared. "I will journey to the castle and arrive right before Dagon and his annoyances reach the gate. I will storm down with my powerful mercenaries at my side, finally killing my dear brother's son and clearing my path to the throne."

"Don't you mean *nephew?*"

"*Ugh!*" Erex replied, rolling his eyes. He jumped out of his chair and flew up to a high window covered by a blue velvet curtain. He slashed the curtain open with one hand, revealing the black night and miles and miles of emptiness. He turned back to the waiting gargoyle. "It is time! Call our friends and tell them that Erex needs a bit of a favor."

"Yes, sir! Yes, sir!" Milton flew to the windowsill beside his master and blew into a strange sounding horn.

"It's time for some revenge," Erex sneered.

41

HOME

At this point Dagon was getting terribly tired of planes or any vehicle that involved rocketing into the sky, especially one piloted by his crazy friend. Needless to say, he loved Maylis dearly, but where there's love, there's often annoyance—at least that's what he told himself. It was still nighttime, although there were no windows to prove his theory. He found his friends asleep in varying awkward positions in the uncomfortable airplane seats. He would have joined them, but the angst and the jittery feeling inside his heart kept his consciousness in full swing. Something about Erex darkened him, the way he moved and carried himself as they fought. It may just have been Dagon's lack of experience, but Erex's moves seemed smoother. He jumped with more agility than anyone Dagon had ever fought before.

Stewing on this subject wasn't going to help him sleep. He got up and paced soundlessly past Aidryan and Chase who were curled up together in the corner. He couldn't help but smile. He walked to the captain's cockpit and pushed the curtains aside to reveal an interesting scene. Maylis sat in the captain's chair with his eyes looking forward, his hands steady on the wheel, and his headset in place. However, Dagon did a double take when he saw Mr. Gobique, the multitalented island man. Mr. G also sat with his headset on but was turned toward Maylis. In his hand was a gooey glazed doughnut. He was tearing off bite-size pieces and feeding them to Maylis at a consistent rate, paying attention to Maylis's eyes and facial expressions to make sure he delivered the treat at the correct pace. There was a crumpled bag on the floor beside them, which obviously contained the doughnuts. Mr. G noticed Dagon's presence and stopped what he was doing.

"Normally, I wouldn't ask," Dagon began. "But I actually want to know."

Mr. Gobique's cheeks turned pink as he carefully put what was left of the doughnut inside the bag and wiped his hands politely on a napkin, which they evidently had on standby.

"Dagon, buddy, whatcha doing?" Maylis stated before Mr. G could explain.

"Apparently having a dream, an extremely weird dream. What exactly is going on here?"

"Nothing, really. I just needed help staying awake. I thought that sugar, some company, and a little caffeine would do the job quite nicely."

"Caffeine?" Dagon asked in a high-pitched voice.

"Yes," Maylis chirped. Dagon looked toward the copilot with big yearning eyes. "G, I think it's time for some coffee. Hit me!"

"Sure thing," Mr. G got up and reached for the carafe.

"It's actually a pretty good system we got going on," commented Maylis.

"Seems like it, but are you sure it's not affecting your steering?"

"What? Do you mean *this* steering?" Maylis turned the wheel abruptly to the left, causing Dagon to grab the cockpit door and disturbing a few people in the back. Dagon could hear Aidryan yelling her head off and Sarina spouting what must have been Laminian curse words. "Looks like everyone's up!" Maylis declared, clearly happy with his success. "Oh, and look at that. So is the sun."

Dagon clambered down the narrow aisle of the plane to announce that they would be landing soon. Surprisingly, Maylis touched down with minimal turbulence. As the plane taxied to a halt, they all cheered and waited for Mr. G to turn off the "Fasten Seatbelt" sign. The door opened, and everyone pushed to get off. Dagon overheard Chase say, "It was totally a real kiss" and Aidryan shooting him down by saying, "It doesn't count. I was forced to because the stupid plane pushed my face into yours." Dagon decided to let them figure it out. He already had his fill of awkward that day.

"Take a look outside, my friends!" Maylis yelled with his arms spread like a majestic eagle. "You are now in your homeland. You are now in the center of Lamin."

Each of them took a moment to gawk. Maylis was home again, and it gave him the warm fuzzies. Mr. Gobique was verbose in his excitement and yakked on about how he'd always wanted to come back and how it was so different now than when he was a kid, *blah, blah, blah*. Dagon, Aidryan, and Zennith had the opposite response. Hardly any words escaped their lips. They were standing in a field filled with winged horses, tickly grass, and beautiful flowers. The delicate breeze filled their noses with the clearest air they had ever breathed. But by far, the most impressive sight was the castle towering above them about a mile away. Even from this distance, Dagon and his friends felt like they could see every detail. They glanced over at each other and smiled deviously. Aidryan tagged Zennith who yelled in protest but then quickly followed suit as she darted across the field. Zennith passed it on to Dagon, Dagon passed it on to Chase, and pretty soon, they were all laughing and dodging each other while Mr. Gobique sat happily on the sidelines, polishing off the last of the doughnuts.

As for Sarina, the feeling she had when she saw the castle was truly indescribable. Her many travels had satisfied her wanderlust, and the thought that she was returning home made her heart swell. This deep joy affected her physical appearance. Her form changed from a plump fifty-year-old to a lithe sixteen-year-old. As she ran toward her friends on that flowered field just as the sun started to peek from behind the castle, Zennith swore she was Rarity, his Rarity. He stopped in his tracks and stared for a while, enjoying her sweet memory. As the game was winding down, Sarina changed back to her middle-aged self. This saddened Zennith, but he got over it when Aidryan pulled out a giant picnic basket she had transformed from a rock. Dagon filled seven tall water glasses and passed them around. They reminisced about their travels and laughed at all the funny experiences, then settled in to make a plan.

It didn't take long for someone to suggest they ride the pegasi to the castle's front gate. Everyone thought it would be a fitting tribute to their dear friend, Rarity. Aidryan approached the closest horse and gently caressed its nose. The horse nuzzled up to her and wrapped her gently in its wings. Zennith attempted to ride a magnificent stallion like a bucking bronco, but it was a docile creature and just stood there chewing a wad of grass and refused to cooperate. Before long, Dagon, Maylis, Mr. G, Chase, and Sarina had selected their rides as well. They lined up together and signaled the release. Seven stunning, snow white pegasi took off into the sky. Zennith and Maylis showed off as they dipped and dove and spun all at the same time. This went on for a while until Chase showed his superiority over them all. He stood upright on his pegasus's back and spread his arms wide while his ride coasted gently on the wind.

"Impressive!" Dagon said. "What do you think, Aidryan?"

She looked at him. "Oh, he's not done yet, cousin. Just wait until the real fun hits."

Dagon watched this foreigner from the North inching ahead. Chase was now front and center. "Get ready!" He called to everyone.

Whoosh. Chase jumped straight up into the air, brought his knees to his chest, and using that momentum, flipped around twice. His pegasus moved into position just in time to catch him. Chase saluted his audience while the crowd erupted in exuberant applause. Even the pegasi were impressed and whinnied their approval. The excitement didn't stop there because just then Aidryan shouted, "Look, the gates of the castle! We finally made it." The wattage of the seven's smiles was enough to power an entire city, and their descent was like riding a roller coaster with no rules or rails. A few moments later, they touched down gracefully on the path leading up to the entrance.

"Dagon, I think you should lead us to the gates," Aidryan suggested.

"After all, you are the stinkin' prince of this joint," Zennith enthused, then apologized to the air in case the king had heard him.

They fell in line behind the prince and walked their mounts toward the impressive gates. Just then, Sarina cried out in surprise as she was dive-bombed right off her pegasus by a flying creature. That was when they looked up. Erex hovered above them, clutching a golden scimitar. He wore the familiar ninja outfit but instead of a black mask, this was solid gold. A hundred cement gargoyles flanked their master in the air, waiting for the signal to attack. Mr. G scooped up Sarina and helped her onto his pegasus. She sat sidesaddle, clutching her arm and silently wishing Erex would get crushed by a meteor.

"Well, isn't this a happy reunion?" Erex laughed sarcastically. "You know you can't get away once you're marked, boy."

Dagon turned his mount to face the enemy. "I am Dagon, prince of Lamin, and this is my domain. You are not welcome here." Dagon lifted his chin to disguise the fact that he was trembling.

"Oh, my dear nephew, I beg to differ." Erex shot a powerful lightning bolt straight into Dagon's chest, knocking him off his pegasus and onto the gravel path. "You recall that I was outnumbered last time, yes? Well, I won't be having that problem again. Am I right, boys?" Erex gave the attack command.

Suddenly, the kids were swarmed by scores of nasty gargoyles. Erex glided past the fighting to where Dagon lay bruised and beaten. "So what shall I do after I destroy you? Oh, I know! Your mother's still alive right? Perhaps I'll visit her and her sister. I'm feeling magnanimous today, so I might spare your dear cousin just long enough to dispatch her in front of her parents. Now that would make for an interesting family gathering."

The sorcerer's taunting inflamed Dagon. The more Erex rambled on, the more incensed the prince became. Dagon's face began to glow until electric blue flames burst from his eyes and engulfed Erex. Every person and gargoyle alike stopped swinging to watch the spectacle. Gradually, the flames sputtered out, revealing a trembling form. There stood Erex, or at least what was left of him. The mighty wizard had been transformed into a child, and his previously large frame was now three feet shorter and scrawny with youth. He wore a pink tutu; a sparkly tiara; and a sash that read, "Drama Queen." No words were exchanged for a solid minute and a half.

Zennith cleared his throat. "Well, that's a new trick."

Erex shuffled uncomfortably. "Looks like I'll be going then, but you haven't seen the last of me." He whistled for his gargoyle and flew off in a prepubescent huff, his sash flapping in the wind.

As the rest of the gargoyles followed, Aidryan heard one of them say, "Man, I hope we still get paid for this job. I got a wife and kids to feed." Aidryan turned and gave Dagon a reassuring smile.

The prince stepped up to the gate and prepared to lift the knocker, but before he could, the doors thundered open, revealing the gilded entrance hall of the castle.

"Home," Dagon whispered.

42

TO BE A KING

The palace boasted soaring ceilings, imposing pillars, and polished marble floors. Extravagant flower arrangements graced every nook and cranny. Lines of exuberant servants dressed to the nines came pouring in to greet them. Aidryan fussed with her hair and tried to smooth the wrinkles from her tattered cloak. Zennith's outward appearance didn't even cross his mind, which was a good thing because he was sporting a nasty case of bed head. Maylis waved and laughed as if he were royalty. Mr. Gobique, Chase, and Sarina backed up so they were out of frame and wouldn't steal the spotlight from their friends.

Horns sounded, and in strode King Klayric. He was quite tall. His hair was dark brown like Dagon's with just a hint of gray creeping in on the sides. He had a kind but careworn face, and his eyes were a striking green. It was obvious they had seen much over the years, both joy and pain. To make this moment even better, the beautiful woman who accompanied him was none other than Nancy Porter, Dagon's mother. She wore a strapless dress in Laminian purple with an intricate pattern of diamonds cascading down one side. To complete the look, a silver tiara rested on her head. Dagon broke from his trance and flew into his mother's arms.

"Does a father earn a hug like that?" the man with the crown inquired.

Dagon stepped back from his mother's embrace and looked up to meet his father's gaze. "Of course he does," he said, his voice rough with emotion.

His father reached down and embraced him. Dagon was at a loss for words. Time went in slow motion as if it were savoring the occasion just as much as he was. Then King Klayric spun him around and announced, "The prince of Lamin has come!" He said it with such gusto that it echoed through the halls and made its way outside startling a flock of sparrows.

Shouts of joy rang out. Small purple and white flowers were thrown from every direction. Some landed in Zennith's hair, and no matter how hard he tried to brush them off, more and more kept flying in. Aidryan stood beside him, laughing and hugging her sides to keep them from bursting. A couple came strolling over to investigate the whereabouts of the hearty laugh.

"Aidryan, please act more ladylike. You are in a castle you know, my dear," the woman scolded.

Aidryan looked over. "Mom? Dad? You're here?"

"Yes, we thought we'd surprise you," her dad said.

"Well, you certainly di—what are you wearing?"

Aidryan's mom flashed a smile. "Oh, this old thing? Now I know you just fought monsters and all, but we need to get you in more suitable attire for the feast." She was putting an outfit together in her head while her husband brushed off their daughter's shoulders, thinking it might help.

Aidryan's eyes gleamed. "There's a feast?"

Oh, there was a feast all right. King Klayric was not known to do things in a small way. The newcomers figured that out very quickly. Each of them was thrown into a room full of "appropriate" clothing choices, hair products, and beauty consultants. In fifteen minutes flat, they were out of their rooms and making their way down the beautiful staircase. Aidryan's dress was navy blue and flowy. She wore her magical hair clip and a stunning silver necklace. Of course, the boys teased her relentlessly until they entered the dining room (and even a little more after that). They were each dressed in suits. Dagon had a purple flower in his buttonhole. Aidryan found Mr. G and asked him something that she had been wondering about for ages.

"So what's with all the purple? The walls in your mansion, Mrs. Porter's dress, and that cloak I found. Does is have some kind of special significance?"

"Oh yes, dear! That wondrous dye is made from a rare Laminian berry. It's made using a very complicated process that's been handed down in the same Laminian family for generations."

"It's beautiful!" said Aidryan.

Dagon caught a glimpse of his father and mother across the room and asked Maylis and Zen to go over with him. Dagon and Zennith clambered in that direction, being especially careful about who or what they could potentially knock over. Maylis, being the pro, helped them navigate and saved a few vases before greeting the king.

"Ah, my boy! Just in time." Klayric raised his glass for a toast. "Ladies and gentlemen of Lamin," he began. "The feast will now commence!"

That sent everyone into a frenzy. People practically ran to the nearest table and sat down all in one motion. Dagon wasn't sure if was because there were not enough seats or the food was just *that* good. When he spotted Zennith zooming in on the seat with the largest plate of tenderloin, his father grabbed both their collars. "As royalty and the royals' confidant," he explained, "we sit at the head table. We don't need to rush because those seats are reserved for us."

After the boys fixed their jacket collars, they followed the king to the head table and sat down. On Dagon's right, Zennith made himself comfortable and was intently staring at a particularly juicy piece of meat. On Dagon's left sat someone he had never seen before. She—yes, *she*—looked his age or a year or two younger (he didn't care) and had pastel-pink hair with light purple eyes. He must have been staring for an abnormally long time to get that much detail from the "first glance."

"Do you think this shade is over the top? I just wanted to do something different, you know?"

Silence.

"Well, is it?"

"Oh . . . uh, yes . . . wait, I mean, no. It looks really cool. Not like cool as in *ice*, but cool as in *good* and cool as in *awesome*. Yeah!"

The girl laughed. "My name is Luna, by the way. I'm a long-time friend of your family's. You don't have to introduce yourself, I know you are Prince Dagon. It's very nice to meet you." She put her hand lightly on his shoulder for just a moment then turned back to her plate and smiled to herself. Dagon scanned the table to make sure no one had witnessed his epic fail of an intro. Luna turned back to face the tomato that was Prince Dagon. She touched his shoulder again and made direct eye contact before speaking. "I've always wanted to know what the world is like beyond the Laminian borders. My parents think I'm too young to venture out, but I'm so past curious. Please tell me. I want to know," Luna begged.

Naturally, Dagon's control over his speech was no barrier once again. He first began to tell her about where he used to live and then moved on to all the places he'd traveled. It felt good to share his voyage and even his hardships with someone other than the people who experienced it with him. It was especially nice to have such an attentive listener. The party had been going on for nearly two hours. At that point, Dagon and the rest of the newbies were too full to move their arms to even reach for more sauce. Klayric seemed to notice the beached whale behavior on the opposite side of the centerpiece and decided to do something about it.

"Son, why don't we step outside for a bit and talk? I want to hear all about your journey to Lamin."

Dagon nodded. He was afraid talking might rip holes in inconvenient places. Luna helped him up, which worsened the situation by 100 percent, but at least he was able to make it up and out alive. His father guided him outside to a soaring balcony overlooking the beautiful field where Dagon had first set eyes on the castle. His father leaned in closer and set his hand firmly on the same shoulder that Luna had at the beginning of the evening. Of course, the result was not the same. Now that he was in an upright position, Dagon felt safe to speak without popping his buttons so he launched into his story for the second time. He noticed that each time it got easier and lost memories resurfaced, and he could laugh at them all over again. Klayric expressed how amazing it was to be reunited with his wife and added some compliments about her that made Dagon uncomfortable but happy. Then Dagon remembered the coins in his pocket. He reached inside and pulled out the five slightly dusty platinum coins.

Klayric laughed. "Good job, son! I knew you would have no trouble finding these treasures."

"Oh, yeah, piece of cheesecake," Dagon answered extra loud, but inside his head he was screaming insults. *Why did you require me and my friends to go to such lengths to find these coins? We could have been killed for heaven's sake. What was the purpose?*

Apparently, King Klayric was a mind reader as well as a powerful ruler. "You know, Dagon, because you came of age and it was time to take on the role of prince, I knew you would benefit from working through the challenges the journey brought you. You and the others had to think on your feet and learn to work together to solve complex problems. Those are necessary skills of an effective leader. Although Erex's timeline for domination is currently—*ahem*—postponed, he will not rest until this throne is his. Knowing your enemy is half the battle." His father studied the coins. "I think these treasures can now be put to different use." Klayric took all five coins in one hand and waved his other hand on top of them. A small powerful glow surrounded them. After Dagon blinked once, four of the coins had shrunk to half their size and were attached to fine platinum chains. Dagon noticed the one with the *L* was missing and inquired about it. "I believe your question will be answered if you inspect the top of your head." Klayric laughed.

Dagon followed his father's instructions and moved his fingers from his forehead up until he touched a hard object. He lifted it off to reveal a stunning platinum crown. "It's beautiful, thank you."

"You're very welcome. But remember, Dagon, love is more important than all the treasure in the world."

Dagon turned to leave the balcony and rejoin the party. The young prince was carrying the four necklaces over his arm and wearing his crown proudly. But when he turned to look at his father, he was stunned to find him not there. Dagon frantically looked around and then spotted someone who hadn't been there before. The man walked up to him and stared directly at his face. It was the peasant from the Laminian outpost. Then the man's face morphed into someone he loved, his father.

Klayric couldn't stop laughing at the dazed look on his son's face. "Had you going, didn't I? Returning the sticky bun was a nice touch, don't you think?"

The king led Dagon back inside as the guests started to migrate into the ballroom. Dagon joined his family and friends. He handed the necklaces to his three companions as a symbol of their Platinums group and hung the fourth around his neck. One conversation led to another. Pretty soon, everyone agreed they would stay in Lamin, perhaps for good. The night was winding down. So much had happened that day that when the sun sunk behind the castle, Aidryan, Maylis, Zennith, and Dagon's eyes were struggling to stay open. Sarina, on the other hand, was chatting happily with Klayric and Nancy. The king seemed delighted to catch her up on what had happened during her time of absence.

Most of the guests had left, and the boys were ready to turn in, but Aidryan was looking for Chase.

"Last time I saw him, Mr. G was teaching him a card trick. That was about fifteen minutes ago," offered Maylis. That was the first sign of everything going horribly wrong. Dagon was sitting with Maylis and Zennith when Zennith started acting strangely.

"What is it, Zennith? What's going on?" asked Maylis.

"It's nothing. I just thought Dagon would still be wearing his crown."

Dagon's hands flew to his head. "You should have said something earlier, buddy, 'cause that's what I thought, too." Everyone panicked. They searched everywhere, but the longer they looked, the more stressed they became. "How the heck could I lose a crown?" Dagon lamented.

"Looking for this?" Dagon froze. The voice was familiar, but the tone was not.

"Aidryan, I think we found Chase."

Aidryan came running from behind a flower embellishment to see for herself but stopped abruptly once she saw Chase. His eyes were black, and there was no light in them. He twirled the crown around in his hands a few times.

"I've always liked surprises!" Chase sneered.

Dagon held his hand out firmly. "Return my crown, Chase."

"Oh, I don't think so. You see, I need this more than you do."

Aidryan couldn't take it anymore. She pulled the hair clip sword out of her hair and pointed it at Chase. "What the heck happened to you? Just give the crown back and fix your eyes!"

"I think I'll pass, but thanks for trusting me, all of you. It made things so much easier. Now I gotta run, someone is waiting for me. He tends to be very impatient."

Chase steered clear of Aidryan's sword but said, "Don't worry, dear. You'll see me again, maybe not as soon as you'd like. But time flies, and so do I." With that, he sprouted wings, soared out the door, and was gone.

EPILOGUE

"Not so fast!" a female voice rang through the air, startling the quiet serenity of the field. She rode a swift pegasus and chased after a man or something the man carried. The man's pegasus was lightning fast and the rider was vastly skilled, which made catching up to him difficult. Suddenly, two more riders appeared behind the woman, which made her urge her mount to fly even faster.

Pegasus riding was a popular sport in the kingdom of Lamin, especially among the king's closest friends. Aidryan, Zennith, and Maylis lived at the palace and enjoyed the fine advantages of being the next best thing to royalty. It had been a decade since the incident with Erex and Chase at the welcome home party. Dagon's crown had been replaced within the week, but the shock of the betrayal lingered on. Aidryan took the longest to recover but bounced back with time. She knew she needed to move on so that was what she did.

Five years ago, the companions faced Chase and Erex again, and it was not a clean fight. Dagon was just days away from ascending the throne when a gargoyle was spotted hovering near the castle. It was captured and interrogated. Now the king knew Erex and his apprentice were spying on them and preparing to wage war. Dagon was just twenty-one at the time, but he led his father's army against Erex and his minions. The losses were great on both sides, but as the sun rose on the second day of battle, the young prince finally overpowered Erex and his evil sidekick, Chase. On the day of his unforgettable coronation, Prince Dagon married his beautiful fiancée Luna and declared it to be the most precious day of his life.

"I would have told it better!" Aidryan scoffed. She crossed her arms and glared at Zennith who claimed that his version made everyone seem valiant and brave. "I beg to differ," Aidryan snapped back.

"Oh, come on, Aidryan. You would have gone into morbid detail about Mr. Psycho and your subsequent road to recovery. Nobody wants to hear about that."

"I wouldn't have done that, I swear!"

"Ten years later, you are still acting like teenagers," Maylis interjected.

"I don't think that's ever going to change. What do you think, my love?" Dagon gazed at his wife.

"I believe you are right, honey," she cooed.

"Love the green hair," Zennith offered.

Luna looked horrified and turned red, making her appear ready for the holiday season. "It was supposed to be blue!"

Maylis put his hands up. "Oh, just calm down, everyone!" He still hated confrontation.

It took everyone a few minutes to settle down, but once they did, they were able to enjoy the delicious packed lunches provided by the royal kitchen.

"To be fair," Dagon said, "you all tell the story perfectly. The little differences make each one unique."

"You're right as usual," Zennith said. He looked at Aidryan, expecting her to say the same thing, but the look in her eyes said otherwise.

"Dagon may be right, but I'm certainly *not* saying Zennith's right. You won't catch me saying that ever!" she declared. Everyone laughed, including Aidryan.

They went back to enjoying the view and recounting stories from their past.

Dagon spoke up. "It was our destiny to go on that journey, and I'm so glad we did. It showed us that what we thought was impossible was actually possible. It pushed us to conquer our fears, and we met some wonderful people and creatures along the way."

"We couldn't have done it without you, man," Zennith said. "You kept us together. Even when we left to follow our own paths, you reminded us that we were meant to be together."

"Agreed," Aidryan said. Looks came from everyone. "What? I didn't say he was right."

"Well, then, let's all agree," Maylis began, "to never leave each other's sides and be together always, to never harm or lie to one another, to always hold each other up, to celebrate our victories, and to comfort each other in our losses."

"We agree!" they all shouted.

And that was what they did.

About the Author

Sophia Borzilleri started writing *Platinums* when she was just twelve years old. She got her inspiration from various fiction writers that inspired her to create her own world. Four years and many edits later, she completed the novel and is excited to share it with you.

About The Illustrator

Kaya Tinsman grew up in quiet and rural Lumberville, Pennsylvania. She attended Pratt Institute in Brooklyn, New York, where she graduated with a Bachelor of Fine Arts degree in painting. While Brooklyn was exciting, she longed for the slower pace of her hometown and the ability to submerge herself in the woods and observe the lives of local fauna. Kaya started the creative business 'Little Gypsy Bones' from which she sells her sterling silver and bone jewelry and wildlife inspired illustrations. Visit her at littlegypsybones.com

CPSIA information can be obtained
at www.ICGtesting.com
Printed in the USA
BVHW070224160219
540444BV00001B/6/P